Far to the east, toward Tribulation, and a little to the south, he glimpsed another figure moving briefly along the crest of a barely noticeable slope. Slade backed down from the knoll.

"They're watchin' the ridges, all right. Looks like Allard might have one bunch of hands sweepin' west from the reservation, and probably another bunch comin' this way from Tribulation. Like circle riders at a roundup."

The deputy swallowed. "They must of passed right over us."

"This time, because we was ridin' the low places. But it shows that Allard means business. If they don't get us this time, he'll just send them back and make them do it over."

Ace Charter Books by Clifton Adams

THE BADGE AND HARRY COLE
ONCE AN OUTLAW/RECKLESS MEN
THE GRABHORN BOUNTY
HARD TIMES & ARNIE SMITH
THE LAST DAYS OF WOLF GARNETT
SHORTY

THE GRABHORN BOUNTY

CLIFTON ADAMS

ACE CHARTER BOOKS, NEW YORK

An Ace Charter Book

Published by arrangement with Doubleday & Co., Inc.

ISBN: 0-441-30223-8

Third Ace Printing: January 1983
Published simultaneously in Canada

Manufactured in the United States of America
Ace Books, 200 Madison Avenue, New York, New York 10016

CHAPTER ONE

I

FRANK SHADE had traveled a long way to get nowhere. He was hot, saddle galled, and mean tempered. He was emptygutted and dehydrated. Sand fleas worked in his Indian-black hair. His beard itched. His grimy clothing had sweated to his raw-boned frame like a second skin.

Somewhere south of the Antelope Hills he had lost Brown's trail—if indeed the trail had ever belonged to Brown. For two days Shade had been blundering westward toward the Cap Rock, grimly ignoring the possibility that the mission was doomed to failure. Telling himself that sooner or later, if he kept pushing, he would cross Brown's trail.

Now he knew that it was wishful thinking. Once again Brown had successfully robbed the Grabhorn Express Company, gravely wounding the already tender pride of the

Grabhorns—not to mention the Choctaw and Canadian Valley Railroad, which company paid Shade's monthly salary.

But at the moment Shade was more concerned with a distant horsebacker than with his own shaky career as a railroader. Ever since his departure from Fort Sill more than a week ago, Shade had felt the breath of the trailer on his neck, but only within the past few hours had the rider grown bold enough to show himself.

Squinting back over his left shoulder, Shade noted that the rider had closed some distance but was still too far away to be much more than a shapeless speck. Indian? That didn't seem likely. The Comanches had had their last big fling in '75—almost four years ago.

Outlaw was more like it. A cautious ridge rider, maybe, with his eye on the two horses.

The thought did nothing to soothe Frank Shade's peeling nerves. He was in strange, hostile country, with only a dim notion of his own location in this rippling sea of brown grass. He grunted with long-building frustration, then climbed down from his claybank gelding and pretended to inspect the gear on the pack animal.

The horsebacker hadn't moved. He was slouched down in the saddle, motionless as stone. The hell with him, Shade thought. He had more important things to think about. Faint-hearted ridge riders would have to take their turn.

He remounted and reined south where he hoped to find a watering place. Damn a country, anyhow, that was naked of landmarks, where one shortgrass knoll looked exactly like a thousand others.

He was a lanky, angular, ungraceful man in his early thirties, with a rawboned face as dour as a Hopi dance mask. Nothing about him suggested weakness. He was as lean as a winter gaunted wolf, tough as the end-of-track shanty towns that he had grown up in. There were times—

rare times—when a stray grin would cross his homely face, and for a moment he would warm like an Irish gandy dancer on payday. But Irish gandy dancers never came to anything. There were places in this country where display of human warmth could be a fatal weakness, and, at one time or another, Shade had lived in most of them.

He was a big man, capable of big emotions. At the moment he was filled with frustration. He was also an ambitious man, and he could feel his ambitions going more sour by the day.

The horsebacker was closing the gap, Shade noticed, after several minutes of aimless travel. When the stranger had closed to less than a thousand yards, Shade reined up a second time and hauled his short-barreled Winchester out of the saddle boot. The man was a gray-whiskered old-timer wearing what appeared to be a cast-off cavalry campaign rig and a buckskin hunting shirt. For footgear he wore blackened buckskin moccasins with trailing Comanche heel tassels.

The animal was a small, bull-nosed, speckle rumped Appaloosa that the old man must have stolen from some Plains Cheyenne, or maybe Arapaho. Next to honor, Indians valued good paints and Appaloosas above all things, so there wasn't much chance that the buckskinned old gaffer had come by the animal legally.

The old man rode slump-shouldered, Indian-like, his stirrups let out full length for his skinny legs. A cavalry .45 in a non-regulation holster was strapped around his middle over the hunting shirt; a fifteen-shot Henry rode in a saddle boot beside his left knee. His whiskers were short and untrained, like the bristles on a wild musk hog. His thinning gray hair was carefully plaited and greased, forming two skimpy braids that barely reached his shoulders. Squaw man, Shade thought.

The old man rode with his bony hands crossed on the

saddlehorn. His faded blue plainsman's eyes regarded Shade with mild interest. At Shade's curt command he reined up, gazing indifferently into the muzzle of the Winchester. "All right, old man, maybe now you'll tell me what you're up to."

The old man shrugged. "Trailin' after you. And a damn-fool business it's been, too, if you was to ask me. I'll tell you the truth, young feller, you've been a tolerable big disappointment to me." He turned his head and spat tobacco juice into the dust-brown grass. "I was over at the trader's store when you landed in Fort Sill. That's how I knowed who you was. Powerful smart feller, Sam Wrinkel says to me—Sam's the trader over at Sill. Works for the railroad over in the Nations, Sam says. That started me to thinkin' . . ." His bleak gaze moved along the blued surface of the Winchester's barrel.

Self-consciously, Shade lowered the muzzle. Then, with a vague, unfocused expression of disgust, he shoved the weapon back into its leather sheath.

"Started me to thinkin'," the old-timer repeated in a conversational tone. "Now what do you reckon a railroader's doin' clean over here in Comanche country? I put the question to Sam Wrinkel, and he don't know. I start on the officers and men, but they don't know either. But the Provost, when I put the question to him, he starts to look a mite queer. Now the Provost, he's a tolerable honest man—for a officer—and honest white men are sorry liars. Can't say why it is. Take a Comanche, or maybe a Kiowa, straight as a war arrow amongst theirselves, but when they're . . ."

The old man shifted his hands on the saddle horn and spat again. "But I guess you ain't interested in Injuns. What you're really interested in is a gent called Brown—ain't I right?"

Frank Shade stared at the weathered old face. He had

planned this campaign in utmost secrecy. Always before, Brown had somehow been forewarned when a posse's net had started to close around him. For reasons that were beyond Shade's understanding, the dirt-poor settlers, the one-mule-farmers would freely and unhesitatingly aid the bandit and killer. This time it was to have been different. This time Shade was to have gone alone after Brown, with no advance advertisement.

But he hadn't counted on his saddle animal going lame. It hadn't seemed like much of a risk, touching at Sill long enough to buy another animal from the civilian trader. But there had been the Provost—there was always something when you went after Brown. The same Provost that Shade had worked with once, on an Army payroll robbery that had involved the railroad. And Wrinkel, the trader, who had recognized Shade from Lord knew where. Now, worst of all, this larcenous old relic, determined, no doubt, to cut himself in on the famous Grabhorn bounty.

But not if Frank Shade had any say in the matter. "Hate to disappoint you, old-timer. But I don't know anybody called Brown."

The old man scratched the Appaloosa's neck. "Damn if I ain't about ready to believe you," he said mildly, "the way you been blunderin' around the prairie since leavin' Sill. It's the lovin' truth, son that you've been a cruel disappointment to me. Big man-tracker, so Sam Wrinkel claimed. Best the railroad had, says he. Pleasant Potter, I says to myself, this here's your chance to see some men-trackin' like she's done by a expert. So . . ." He spread his hands innocently. "There I was, not doin' a thing but loafin' around Sam's store. . . ." He glanced at Shade, the pale eyes coming to sharp focus.

"So," Shade said with weighty sarcasm, "you just decided to trail along."

Behind the whiskers the puckered mouth almost grinned. "That's about the size of it."

"Never givin' a thought, of course, to the Grabhorn bounty money."

The pale eyes lost their sharpness and became vague. "It ain't the bounty I want, son. Not much of it, anyhow—just enough to make it look decent."

Shade lowered his gaze hoping the old man wouldn't see the craftiness behind his next question. "Don't reckon you'd be acquainted with Brown, would you, old-timer?"

Pleasant Potter shifted sides with his tobacco cud and wiped his mouth. "Nope."

"Maybe, then, you've got a notion where he's hidin' out?"

"Not that neither," the old man said mildly. "Don't know a thing about the jaybird, 'cept his specialty's robbin' Grabhorn Express cars 'n coaches. And up to now nobody's ever laid a hand on him." Again he looked at Shade, almost smiling. "Nobody. Includin' you, son."

Shade could feel his face burning. Nobody had to tell him that, as the railroad's prize troubleshooter, this nobody of an express robber had made him look foolish at every turn. This old-timer was beginning to interest him.

"What makes you think you could earn any part of that bounty money, old man?"

"Well, for one thing, I know this country. You don't."

"What else?"

"I know the folks. Injuns and whites alike. They'll talk to me. They wouldn't to you."

"If you're so sure about all this"—Shade could hardly keep the sneer out of his voice—"why don't you go after Brown yourself, and take all the bounty?"

Pleasant Potter sighed. "Because I ain't as young as I used to be. And I don't get around so good any more, after pickin' up a little touch of frostbite a few winters back."

THE GRABHORN BOUNTY

Shade didn't have to remind himself that he could have had his pick of the best detectives the railroad could hire. But detectives had been no use before, and this time Shade had been determined to do the job alone. An old man would just slow him down. Still, if he knew the country as well as he claimed . . .

Suddenly, Shade looked at the old man and grinned without a hint of mirth. Brown's trail had disappeared almost four days ago. The bandit had vanished as he always had, without a trace, and Shade had kept blundering on to the west out of brute stubbornness.

The old man regarded the indecision with interest. "If it's splittin' the bounty that's frettin' you, forget about it. I get my pension from the government every month. I don't need or want your bounty."

Shade studied him with suspicion.

"There's things more important 'n money," Potter said softly.

Shade found himself nodding. "Like what?"

The old man scratched his bristling chin. "Son, if I got to tell you a thing like that I might as well do it in Comanche, because you wouldn't understand me."

Shade felt himself relax. He almost smiled, realizing that no other answer would have satisfied him. "The trail's four days cold, and the man we're after—sometimes I think he's more ghost than man." He hesitated. Then, because he had nothing to lose, "We could backtrack to the place where the trail broke off, and take another look."

The old man nodded soberly. Shade had the feeling that somewhere behind those whiskers that puckered mouth was grinning. But the eyes were pale and expressionless.

THE GRABHORN BOUNTY

II

With Pleasant Potter leading the way, they returned to the place where Shade had lost Brown's trail. The campsite was in a clearing of mullein, on the bank of some nameless creek, only a few miles west of the Chickasaw Nation.

The old man inspected the area on horseback. Frostbite had taken his toes and part of one heel, and he could walk no more than a few steps without the aid of crutches, which he refused to use. He poked in the ashes of the dead campfire, grumbling, mumbling to himself. He kneed the little Appaloosa down the clay creekbank, scouting upstream and downstream.

"You can make some coffee while I take a little look-see," he had told Shade, returning from his downstream scout. "Like as not we'll be headin' into gyp water country tomorrow. This'll be the last fit coffee we'll get for a spell."

Shade had learned a few things in the two days that they had been together. Scouting was Pleasant Potter's profession; he had spent the best part of a lifetime scouting for the Army, until frostbite had pensioned him off. He reminded Shade of an old Kiowa warrior, too young to die and too old for war. But Pleasant Potter, in one important particular, differed from the Indian. He was a tracker, a man hunter—it was what he knew how to be, and he meant to be one until he died.

From the creekbank Shade could see him now, mumbling to himself, mulling over skirmishes and battles of Indian campaigns that had long since gone into history, while those sharp old eyes scanned the water's edge for sign. For the first time since leaving Sill, Shade began to feel that all was not lost. In an entirely different way, tracking down Brown was as important to the old man as it was to Shade. Pleasant Potter also had his pride. He didn't want to die without it. He didn't want to be forgotten. These were weaknesses and hungers that Shade could understand.

Shade thought about it. It was just possible that joining forces with Pleasant Potter was the smartest thing he had ever done. It was Frank Shade's name that would go on the report to the company—he didn't mind if the old man got some of the credit, unofficially. He wasn't as greedy as all that.

Of course, there was always the chance that this was not Brown's camp at all. A chance, even, that he had been on the wrong trail from the start and that his whole plan for catching Brown was wrong.

Shade staked the animals, got a small stewer from his pack rig and fetched reddish water from the creek. He started a fire, ladled crushed Arbuckle's into the stewer and set it over the flame.

The old man rode up to the fire, climbed laboriously from the saddle, hobbled a short distance and sat on the ground. The Indian-trained Appaloosa stood in its tracks.

Shade demanded, "Well?"

The old scout shrugged and rubbed his tender feet. "You right sure the feller that camped here is the big bank robber you're after?"

Shade's voice remained normal. "If my theory about him is right, it was him. If it's wrong . . . Well, that won't make any difference now.".

"This theory of yours. What's it like?"

Shade almost closed his eyes in concentration. How did you describe a man you'd never seen? He didn't even know the bandit's name. They called him Brown because, at first, the Grabhorn detectives pegged him as a stagecoach bandit known as Shotgun Brown. But that Brown was long since dead, killed over a year ago in Kansas. The express bandit was still called by the same name for the sake of convenience.

The theory. Up in Baxter Springs, at division headquarters, it had sounded reasonable. With the help of the railroad and the Grabhorns' private detectives, he had carefully gathered and organized every scrap of information that might relate to the robberies. All available facts, and even rumors, he had meticulously charted on a territorial map, searching for a pattern that might tell him something about the man known as Brown.

Shade said slowly, "I don't think robbin' express coaches is Brown's regular line of business. I doubt that he's ever had any trouble with the law before—until he started bustin' open express company safes as a regular thing."

The old scout snorted. "I could of told you that much soon's I saw the camp. This feller—Brown, I guess I'll have to call him—he come ridin' toward the creek right over the top of that far ridge." He pointed. "Right here, in the most likely spot for miles around, and not more than a quarter mile from a hard-used Comanche travois trail, he sets up camp. He ain't got a worry in the world, if I can still read signs." Potter shook his head, obviously puzzled. "A mighty queer duck for a famous outlaw. About as cat-footed as a breachy range cow bustin' through a mesquite fence. You sure this is the right feller?"

"If it ain't," Shade said grimly, "I've wasted twenty years workin' for the railroad and learnin' the business. Because I ain't goin' to have a job if I go back to Baxter Springs empty handed."

The old man squinted thoughtfully. "There ain't much left in the way of sign. Looks like he might of crossed the creek upstream a piece. If he did, luck was ridin' with him. The creek's been on the rise. No tracks. Like as not he struck west and lost his tracks for good on the travois trail—even a greenhorn, I reckon, would of thought to do that."

So far Shade hadn't learned a thing. "Is that all?"

"Not quite." From inside his hunting shirt Potter drew a plug of lint-covered tobacco. With his skinning knife, which he carried in a leather sheath on the left side of his gunbelt, he carved off one brown corner and popped it into his mouth. "Tell me somethin'. If this feller is actual the Brown you're lookin' for, and if he's actual as green and ignorant as I think he is, how'd he ever manage to rob folks like the Grabhorns without gettin' his fool self caught?"

Shade moved the boiling coffee off the fire and grinned sourly. "Maybe it's partly because he *is* green and ignorant. Lawmen, bounty hunters, detectives, we've all been lookin' for an experienced hardcase . . . maybe that's where we made our mistake."

The old scout studied on that for a moment, working his tobacco slowly. "There has to be more'n that. There's a limit to brute luck, even for a greenhorn."

Maybe. But sometimes Shade doubted it.

"He makes friends," Shade went on, after a moment's hesitation, almost as though he were afraid of hearing his theory spoken. "Wherever he goes he makes powerful friends who protect him."

Pleasant Potter gazed diplomatically into the distance.

"It's my theory," Shade said wearily, "that Brown don't keep the money he takes off the Grabhorns. I think he gives it away."

The scout stared at him with those pale eyes. "Why would he want to do a fool thing like that?"

"I don't know." How many times had Shade asked himself the same question? "I only know that wherever there's been a Grabhorn robbery, somewhere in the neighborhood there's a sudden spell of prosperity that can't be accounted for in any reasonable way."

Thoughtfully, the old man shifted his cud, spat, and wiped his mouth. "That what brought you clean over here to Comanche country? Somebody come down with a fit of prosperity?"

"Widow woman livin' over with the Choctaws. Her husband had a little leased outfit, raised some corn and ran a few Indian shorthorns. He died last year, leavin' his wife with three younguns and a hatful of debts. Just when she was about to lose everything, all of a sudden she paid off the debts and hired two Indian hands to look after the livestock and work the corn."

"Right after a Grabhorn holdup?"

Shade nodded. "Then over on the Washita, in Chickasaw country, a family came down with the slow fever. Dead broke, far as anybody knew, but all of a sudden they had money for doctorin' and hirin' farm help till they was up and around again." He sloshed a little cold water into the coffee to settle the grounds. He poured the black liquid into tin cups and passed one to the old man.

"A regular do-gooder," Potter said, sampling the brew without bothering to remove his tobacco.

"Except when he's killin' folks with that shotgun that he always carries." Shade's mouth stretched in one of his mirthless grins. "Anyhow, I've been followin' this string of 'good deeds' clean across the Chickasaw Nation and halfway across the Comanche and Arapaho reservation before my saddle animal pulled up lame."

"Don't reckon these folks that come down rich was in too big a hurry to tell you where the money come from."

Shade merely grunted.

"Maybe if you'd of dangled a little bounty money in front of their noses."

16

Shade snorted impatiently. "I told them about the bounty. Ten thousand dollars. More money than most of them could even imagine. They just grinned at me. He's got these people charmed, like a snake charmin' a settin' hen."

Pleasant Potter finished his coffee and lay back on one elbow, his eyes almost closed. "Sounds like a real interestin' kind of feller," he said at last. "Puts me in mind of old Satank, head man of the Kiowas back in seventy-three . . ." His thoughts drifted. For a few minutes he was in another time, another place. He was Chief Scout Potter with ten top-notch Osage trailers under his command. Chief Scout. A man of importance. Army brass, like Little Phil Sheridan, asking him for his opinion. Even Yellow Hair Custer, loud and brash as a peyote drum, shut up to listen when Chief Scout Potter had something to say.

For a moment Shade thought the old man had dropped off. Then he saw the shrunken mouth moving, heard the old man mumbling, talking to himself. "There we was, of a dark November mornin', cold as a well-digger's rump and the snow still comin' down. And that scrubby little mounted band started playin' 'The Girl I Left Behind Me,' which was a lot of damn foolishness because there wasn't a woman within fifty miles of camp. But that was Custer for you. Well, my Osages looked around at one another, then hunched down in their blankets. I told Yellow Hair plain as day there wasn't a man alive could find his way on that prairie in a blizzard, not even an Osage. He just laughed. He was a gutsy little bastard—you got to give him that much. He set the course hisself by compass, and off we started in a rattle of steel and a lot of snortin' and stampin' from the horses, headin' for what Yellow Hair hoped was the Cheyenne camp, somewheres on the Washita . . ."

Shade reached around the fire and took the old man's shoulder. "Potter, you all right?"

17

Potter opened one eye wide and gazed coolly at Shade. "Course I'm all right."

"You was talkin' kind of funny."

He opened both eyes and sat up. "What I was talkin' about," he said stiffly, "was Gen'rl Sheridan's campaign, the one that Custer took charge of, back in . . ." He looked stunned when he counted up the years and found that it had been so long ago. "Back in sixty-eight," he said wonderingly. "And it wasn't funny, son. They wasn't a funny thing about it."

III

Shade built up the fire and fried bacon and cornbread and heated canned beans, all taken from supplies in his pack rig. Shade was faintly amused at the old man's snort of derision. According to Potter's way of thinking, all a man needed in a way of camping equipment was a good gun, coffee, and maybe a skillet.

This brought Pleasant's mind back to that cold trail of Brown's, which wasn't so cold after all, to a scout who knew his business. Even the cold, windblown ashes of a week-old fire had things to tell. In Potter's mind, Brown was shaping up to be even more of a greenhorn than Shade. He was the kind of man that would probably carry canned tomatoes and beans with him, if he could get them. But there were no empty cans at the campsite. No bacon scraps of grease, no trace of cornmeal, not even any discarded coffee grounds. There were a few delicate bones of a sage hen that the camper had roasted over the coals, and partially melted lead pellet from a shotgun charge.

Casually, Potter brought these observations to Shade's attention. "What do you make of it?"

"Looks like Brown—if it *was* Brown—was pretty low on supplies when he camped here."

"That give you some kind of a notion?" the old scout pressed.

"Maybe." Shade grinned to himself, seeing through Potter's lack of confidence in railroad detectives. "I figure he's headed for the nearest town to stock up on supplies. Where *is* the nearest town?"

The old man grunted and spat. "Only town between here 'n Texas is a place called Tribulation, down in what Texas folks call Greer County." He studied Shade's narrow look. "Peers like the gover'ment surveyors never quite got it straight which was the main bed of Red River, the North Fork that trails off not far from Mobeetie, or the Prairie Dog Town Fork that stretches across the biggest part of the Panhandle. You know about Greer County?"

Shade nodded.

"Well," the old man went on, deciding to tell him about it anyway, "there she sets, and a good-sized piece of country too, between them two forks of the Red. Texas organized it and made it a county, but it don't belong to her, accordin' to the gover'ment people in Washington City. It ain't Injun Territory, neither, so they claim. I guess it's no place at all, when you get right down to it. Nobody there but a few hardscrabble farmers claimin' squatter's rights. And a few outlaws over from the Panhandle." He chewed thoughtfully. "There ain't much law in Greer County. The sheriff at the county seat, and maybe a roamin' deputy. There's just the squatters, and the high riders. And the citizens of Tribulation. And a few cowhands that drift over from the Kiowa-Comanche reservation where Texas cowmen rent grass from the Injuns. . . ."

"How far is it to Tribulation?"

Pleasant Potter gazed out at the brown prairie. "Day's ride, thereabouts. We'll camp here tonight and get a early start tomorrow."

IV

They were up at first light, striking west, and late that afternoon they reached the nearly dry North Fork of the Red. They paused in midstream, splashing themselves with iron-red water, as bitter to the taste as the black herb draught of a Kiowa witch woman. It was a stark, hostile country—the land of "gyp water and mesquite soil," as the squatters called it.

"This feller, Brown. Ain't his speciality robbin' railroads?" the old man asked.

"And Grabhorn Express cars."

"Don't it 'peer to you he's ventured a mite far from his stand? I mean, there ain't no railroad for maybe seventy, eighty miles, and no express cars. When he ain't robbin', does Brown always stray this far from his huntin' grounds?"

The same question had nagged at Shade for some time. "He disappears someplace. And I've seen worse places for a man that's lookin to get hisself lost."

Pleasant Potter scratched his bristling chin. "On the other hand, maybe he aims to go out of the express robbin' business."

Shade laughed harshly. "With his record of successful holdups?"

They struck west again, into the dazzling glare of the lowering sun. They rode with their hats pulled down over their eyes. Shade was saddle sore and tired. For the moment his thoughts were limited to soft beds and hot bath water, which he hoped to find in Tribulation. He was vaguely aware of the grassy rise off to his right, and the clusters of thorny mesquite that partially covered the slope, but he noticed no hint of movement. He didn't even hear the sound of the rifle until after the bullet had carried away a sizable piece of his cantle.

CHAPTER TWO

I

"HELL'S AFIRE!" Pleasant Potter said hoarsely, rolling out of his saddle with the strange, limp grace of a Comanche. Shade's reaction came an instant later as he felt himself silhouetted alone and naked against the shaggy monotony of the prairie. Shade's early "cut and shoot" schooling of territorial train camps came to his aid. The first law of self-preservation was "get out of the line of fire."

Showing little of the old scout's grace, Shade grabbed for his short-barreled Winchester and dived for the ground. He landed heavily on his shoulder, grunting, cursing, scrambling toward a clump of mesquite. Another bullet burned a blue-hot hole in the late afternoon, and Shade had the uneasy feeling that the hole had gone right over the top of his empty saddle where he had been sitting.

21

His claybank gelding reared, startled at the bee-like sound of bullets in flight. The animal, finding its reins dangling, broke for the far side of the bushwhacker's slope. The dun pack animal followed awkwardly at a distance. Shade groaned to himself. Meeting up with bushwhackers seemed like trouble enough for one day—he didn't relish this added plague of being set afoot.

A third bullet whipped through the mesquite inches above Shade's head. A twisted branch snapped like brittle bone, bringing down a shower of dry twigs on Shade's back. Near the crest of the slope he saw the puff of gunsmoke before the prairie wind carried it away. He sighted quickly and squeezed the trigger, enjoying the hard, businesslike kick of the Winchester against his shoulder.

Off to Shade's right the old scout had squirmed, flattened like a badger in the short brown grass, to an outcrop of sandstone. Pleasant Potter too had seen the bushwhacker's smoke. The sharp, hostile bark of the Henry joined with the throatier voice of the Winchester. Not that either of them expected to hit anything. But it would give the bushwhacker something to think about.

Suddenly there was silence on the prairie. After a moment Shade rolled over on his back and began reloading. Behind the outcrop, the old scout was doing the same.

"Friend of yours?" Potter called dryly.

"Maybe. . . ." Shade finished reloading and rolled back on his belly, gazing up at the silent slope. "A very valuable friend, maybe."

"You figure Brown give up his scatter-gun for a rifle?"

Shade grunted. "I don't know of anybody else in these parts that would want to kill me." Several seconds passed. They studied the slope with cautious eyes. "What do you think, Potter?"

"Peers like he's cleared out," the scout called. "Hard to

22

tell about drygulchers, though. Think maybe I'll just rest here a spell and see what happens."

Shade studied the slope. Could it be that, after all this time, he and Brown were only a bullet's flight apart?

"There he goes," Potter said, his tone bordering on indifference. He indicated a feathery wisp of dust rising from the far side of the slope. "And a mighty pore excuse for a killer, too, if you was to ask me."

"Good enough for *my* satisfaction," Shade muttered, rising slowly behind his fragile cover of branches. "Keep me covered with that Henry," he told the scout. "I'll go up and take a look-see."

"Be a waste of time," Potter said. "The backshooter's halfway home by this time—wherever that happens to be. Tribulation itself ain't much more'n a jump 'n a holler from that ridge."

"Just the same," Shade said grimly, "I'd kind of like to have a look."

The old man shrugged and obligingly covered the ridge with his rifle. Shade tramped cautiously up the grassy slope. His claybank gelding and pack animal were nowhere in sight. Potter's Appaloosa was grazing peacefully less than a hundred yards away, but the Indian animal shied suspiciously when Shade moved in its direction.

"Don't take much to white folks," the old scout said placidly. "Figures they can't be trusted. Somethin' he learned from Comanches, more'n likely."

Shade continued to the ridge afoot.

It didn't take long to locate the place where the rifleman had been. A brass cartridge case caught the direct rays of the western sun, glittering like a diamond in the brown grass. Shade picked up the case and studied it thoughtfully. A .44 caliber, rimfire. So the bushwhacker had been using a Henry—1860 model, more than likely—the same as the old scout carried. That was a little out of the ordinary. Not many men carried Henrys as personal weapons nowadays: the odd-sized ammunition was too hard to come by.

Shade gazed to the west where the rifleman had disappeared into the sun. He hadn't picked this particular spot, with the sun at his back, by accident.

Shade turned and studied the rifleman's nearly perfect field of fire. "Now," he thought aloud, "if he'd waited awhile and got us in shotgun range, the story might of been a lot different."

Shade tramped back down the slope and showed the cartridge case to the old scout. Potter glanced at it and shrugged. "They's a lot of Henrys."

"But not too much ammunition. You've got an Army trader to keep you supplied, but where would a train robber go to stock up on these .44s?"

The old man shrugged again.

"Brown's the only man I know of in these parts that would go out of his way to kill me. Except, of course, a common high rider that aimed to shoot us and take our horses and plunder. But would an experienced killer be carryin' a Henry?"

The scout placidly chewed his cud. "Nope," he said finally. "I reckon not." He called to the Appaloosa, making clucking, Indian sounds in his throat. The animal lifted its head and huffed, as if testing the air for danger. Satisfied that the trouble had passed, the Appaloosa ambled toward the old man.

II

It didn't take Potter and the Indian pony long to round up Shade's straying animals. Shade, feeling that he was on the right track at last, was eager to get started. He was certain the bushwhacker had been Brown, just as he was now certain that, for one reason or another, Brown had chosen a place called Tribulation to hole up in between Grabhorn robberies.

"No call to break down the animals," Pleasant Potter cautioned as Shade set a brisk pace toward the south. "If the bushwhacker's really Brown, he'll be waitin' for us in Tribulation, I expect."

Which was true enough, Shade had to admit. Brown was a careful man. He never started a thing that he didn't aim to finish—and the killing of an overly curious railroad detective was not likely to be an exception to that rule.

At a slower pace, they reached the north-south mail road a few minutes before sundown. "How much farther?" Shade asked.

"Fifteen, twenty minutes," the old man said, "if you don't care about the horses. Little less'n a hour, if we take it gentle."

A few minutes one way or the other didn't matter now. After all this time. "You set the gait, old man. Like you say, whenever we get to Tribulation, likely Brown will be somewheres close by."

A soft prairie night settled on the two riders. From time to time the old man would glance at Shade, then grunt to himself and spit a stream of tobacco juice into the reddish dust of the mail road. "Mighty pore excuse for a road," he mumbled accusingly to himself. The thought wandered aimlessly in his mind. "I seen Cheyenne travois trails that was better," he blurted. Then, in a quiet, thoughtful vein, "Course, I seen *worse* roads, too, in my day. Take that mud wagon road from the Choctaw Nation to Sill, that the Army used to haul their stores over. . . ."

Given a quiet moment, the old scout's thoughts returned to the days that used to be, when Potter had been a name to reckon with and Comanche had been a word to chill men's blood. Now he was just an old man that nobody remembered, and "Comanche" was just another blanket Indian hanging around trading posts or border towns like Tribulation, throwing his "grass money" away at three-card monte or maybe spending it with the local druggist for Electric Bitters, or some other patent medicine with a high alcoholic content, because it wasn't often that he could find a white man to sell him whiskey.

"Now you take Custer," Potter mumbled to no one at all. "Shore, he was a brassy little dude, but they wasn't a man ever lived that old Long Hair wouldn't stand right up and spit in his eye—you got to give him that!"

Sooner or later—and usually sooner, Shade had observed —the old man's ramblings returned to that bloody day-long fight back in '68 that had come to be known as the Battle of the Washita. Shade was learning to listen, or not listen, as he pleased. It made no difference to Potter.

This time Shade turned his thoughts inward. It had been a long time since he had given much thought to the Frank Shade of twenty-odd years ago. He did so now, because it all had to do with what he was today and what he hoped to be in the future. It also had to do with this search for an express robber which had become an obsession with him.

Borrowing from the old scout's magic, Shade let himself move freely back in time. He could almost hear the ring of steel on steel, the sound of railroad building, the music of his childhood. He could squint his eyes a little, peering through the gathering prairie darkness, and almost see one of those end-of-track shanty towns. In his mind he saw the careless litter of shacks beside the railroad, hovels of sheet iron and waste lumber and bars of canvas and cardboard, build to last only a few days or possibly weeks, until the camp picked up and moved on with the end-of-tack. Boy and young man he had known hundreds of such camps; they had been the only homes he had ever known.

Even as a boy he had hated them. Hated the sloppiness of the alleylike streets, the sullen violence of the people, the drunkenness, the gabble of immigrant tongues. Hating it, but realizing even now, that much of it had rubbed off onto him. He would never be a polished "Company Inspector," not in a thousand years, no matter how he tried. But he had risen many wide cuts above the shanty-town level of his childhood. That was something. And he meant to rise higher. All that stood in his way was a faceless, nameless, shapeless wraith known only as Brown.

Viewed in a certain grim light, the situation could become almost laughable. Frank Shade, the coldly efficient, professional troubleshooter having all his ambitions threatened by a nobody of an amateur badman!

Frank Shade was not laughing. The road to his present respected position had not been a smooth one. He had gathered bruises and wounds along the way, starting as water boy at the age of nine, learning to read by studying illustrations and texts of *The Police Gazette* and occasionally a *Harper's Weekly*. He had been a section boss at the age of nineteen—a near miracle. Long since his mother had died of the "slow fever," his father of hard work and bad whiskey.

With his wits and his fists and an expertness with weapons, he captured the notice of certain officials of the Choctaw and Canadian Valley Railroad. It had been decided that Frank Shade possessed certain qualities which could be used to benefit of the Line.

He was put to riding shotgun in express cars. He also guarded shipments of unusual value for certain stagecoach and express companies with which the Choctaw and Canadian Valley was connected. The officials who had recommended him had made no mistake. Shade's toughness, ambition, and ability with guns all worked to the advantage and profit of the company. He advanced rapidly through the several positions of inspector to his present assignment as troubleshooter. Reasonably enough, Shade assumed that if his successes continued, he would someday soon be advanced to a truly responsible position at Division Headquarters.

Those had been heady days, his future assured. He could now afford to rent a hotel room by the month, whether he was there or not. In the imposing mahogany wardrobe of his room there hung two good business suits and a black greatcoat with a fur collar, besides several changes of pants and shirts and odd coats.

Heady days indeed, Shade thought now, with a grim set to his lantern jaw. The water boy had come a long way. Once while visiting end-of-track on business he had walked among the sweating roustabouts and gandy dancers, wondering if anybody would recognize him. Nobody did. That's how far Frank Shade had come.

Now it was all in the past. As dead as old Pleasant Potter's days of glory on the Washita. And his future would be as dead as his past if he returned to Headquarters without Brown.

THE GRABHORN BOUNTY

III

As a town with a future, there wasn't much to be said for Tribulation. The place consisted—as nearly as Shade could tell—of five business houses and a wagon yard. The business houses were frame shacks haphazardly constructed with green cottonwood lumber called "rawhide." Yellow lamplight beamed through the wide cracks in the warped timbers.

Only two business houses were doing business. Reining east toward the wagon yard, Shade watched a storekeeper load a ranch supply wagon. The wagon was backed up to a front door loading ramp—above the door the place confessed to being the SQUARE DEAL STORE, GEN. MERCHANDISE. The other place doing business was the TEXAS BAR, next door, where two visiting cowhands idled over a bottle.

"Told you there wasn't much to it," Pleasant Potter reminded Shade, indicating the town with a carefully aimed jet of tobacco juice.

Shade grunted. The smell of dirt-poor poverty was about the place. If his theory about Brown wasn't completely haywire, this is just the kind of place the outlaw would choose to hide in.

To the south of the wagon yard, at a distance of about three hundred yards, several cones of light glowed in the darkness. "Comanches?" he asked the scout.

"Or Kiowas," the old man said. "Or maybe Plains Apache. They drift over from the reservation to tank up on patent medicine and play monte." There was a sadness in the old scout's words. He remembered another time, not so long ago.

29

He still lived with names like Kicking Bird, Big Tree, Satank, Quanah. Powerful leaders, fierce soldiers burning with pride. The pride was missing now. They could no longer make war, and most of them refused to learn anything else. It was a sad, bitter thing.

The scout looked at Shade. "You still figure to find Brown in Tribulation?"

Shade nodded. The feeling that Brown was nearby was getting stronger all the time.

"How do you aim to root him out?"

"I ain't sure yet. Sometimes you have to play your hunches and wait for the other man to make his play."

"He takes another crack at bushwhackin'," the old man said dryly, "maybe we won't have to worry ourselves about how we're goin' to spend all that bounty."

They rode on to the wagon yard, which was the end of the one-sided street. "Well . . ." Potter pointed with his chin. "There's our hotel."

The wagon yard was all haywire and rawhide, like the rest of the town. The corral was an enclosure of black-jack poles and rawhide fencing. There was a brush arbor shed, a few stalls, four small bunk shacks, and an extra shack where the stableman lived and stored his feed.

The stableman, whose name was Ludlow Finch, came out of his shack when they dismounted. "Bunk shack's fifty cents a night, if that's what you're after."

Shade nodded. "And corn for the horses, if you've got it. Oats, if you haven't."

"It'll be oats. And another four bits."

Not one to stand on ceremony, Pleasant Potter pulled his rifle and warbag off the Appaloosa and hobbled off toward the nearest bunk. Shade paid for the bunkhouse and boarding the horses. "Where can I get a hot bath?"

"Nowheres," the stableman said bluntly. "Not tonight."

A long, dry, humorless man with the squint of greed in his eyes, Finch studied his new guest. "They's a pump," he said speculatively, "over at the horse trough in the corral. I guess the animals won't mind if you use it."

A cold bath in a horse trough was better than no bath at all.

"That'll be a quarter extra."

Shade's eyes narrowed. "I can see now why you've got such a thrivin' town here. It's the hospitality."

"Soap'll be another dime," said Ludlow Finch, always thinking ahead.

Shade sighed to himself and paid. Then he stripped the claybank and Potter's Appaloosa, removed the pack from the dun and plodded toward the bunk shack.

Potter, fully dressed, was already sound asleep in the lower of the stacked bunks. The Henry rifle lay beside him, the scout's right hand firmly on the walnut grip. Shade brought the two saddles inside and put them in the corner on the plank floor. Methodically, he started going through his roll, looking for clean b.v.d.'s and a shirt.

The old man opened one eye. "The stableman know anything about Brown?"

"I didn't ask," Shade said grimly. "Afraid I didn't have the money to pay for the information."

Potter moved this thought ponderously around in his mind and at last decided that it meant nothing. "What you doin'?" he asked, as Shade gathered his change of clothing.

"Fixin' to take a bath that I've already paid for."

"Damn foolishness," the old scout said placidly. "I heard tell of folks that plain killed theirselves takin' baths in gyp water. Clogged up the pores and they couldn't sweat."

IV

Finch's soap was yellow lye and strong enough to dissolve mesquite root. But Shade applied it liberally, taking satisfaction in the thought that it was as hard on the sand fleas as it was on him.

The few animals in the corral backed off cautiously and watched the strange spectacle with dim interest. Darkness lay heavily on the dreary huddle of shanties that was Tribulation, assuring Shade of privacy. He stripped down to his b.v.d.'s, ducked his head into the trough and lathered his hair and beard with the lye soap. Working quickly, he peeled off the b.v.d.'s, lathered thoroughly, pumped fresh water into a canvas bucket and dumped it over his head. The iciness of the water took his breath away, but he repeated the procedure three times, lathering and rinsing, before drying himself on the tail of the clean shirt.

Shade pulled on a clean pair of socks and b.v.d.'s and stamped into his boots. He lathered his beard once more in the cold water, then, soldier fashion, he began shaving with his eyes closed, by feel.

For the first time since leaving Fort Sill, he felt reasonably clean. No beard to itch, no crawling things in his hair. It was a pleasant sensation. Dignity and self-confidence were rare virtues among the unwashed—this much he had learned as a boy in the railroad camps. Now he could think about Brown without so much urgency. He could consider his own future as a railroader and the prod of desperation was not so persistent.

Then, as he began pulling on his pants, a burst of laughter came from the far end of the corral, near the horses. It was more of a cackle than laughter, a hard, high-pitched sound, like a circle saw biting into a pine knot.

For an instant Shade froze. Then he grabbed for his .45, which he had placed on the edge of the horse trough. In the darkness he fumbled, knocked the revolver spinning. There was a splash. Shade's insides seemed to sink, as the .45 was submerging in the murky water.

CHAPTER THREE

I

A BULKY FIGURE moved toward him along the rawhide fencing of the corral. Was it Brown? Was this the way it was to end? With Shade half naked, unarmed—with a cloud of ridiculousness hovering over the proceeding. It had been ridicule, Shade remembered, that had caused the Grabhorns to post the huge bounty. Ridicule could be a cruel and fearful thing—especially so for men of ambition and pride.

The laughter sounded again. For one crazy moment Shade thought that it was the voice of a woman. But what woman would stand calmly at a corral fence watching a man bathe?

"Damnedest thing I ever seen!" The words came out as a gleeful whoop. And it *was* a woman's voice. Shade felt himself burning, almost glowing with embarrassment. He almost wished the figure in the darkness had been Brown.

33

He struggled to get into his pants and the woman continued to chuckle. "Damnedest thing! Full-growed man, naked as a jaybird, splashin' in a horse trough. Say, whajer doin' in there anyhow, Mr. Jaybird?"

Shade cursed fervently. The boots were on his feet, and the spurs were on the boots, and he couldn't pull his pants on over the spurs. There was nothing for it but to sit down on the edge of the trough, laboriously work the boots off his feet, pull on his faded California pants, then stamp once again into his tight-vamped footgear.

The woman fell into another fit of laughter, hanging to a blackjack post for support. Shade shrugged into his clean shirt, punching the wet tails into his pants. He fished almost shoulder deep in the trough for his gun. He tried to ignore the woman as he began to dry the revolver on the discarded shirt—but she would not be ignored. She continued to howl throughout the ordeal.

At last Shade moved stiffly toward the fence. Suddenly the laughter stopped. "Lookie here, I was just funnin' you a mite. Ain't no call to go gettin' your hackles up." Nervously, she eyed the .45 in Shade's hand.

Shade was now close enough to see her clearly. He was looking at a round, doughy face from which small, dark eyes studied him shrewdly, without a trace of merriment. The woman herself was short, thick, with the figure of an oak stump. A cotton dress drooped in tentlike folds about the shapeless figure. Shade guessed her age in the middle forties, but he could have been wrong by ten years in either direction.

Reluctantly, Shade shoved his damp .45 into his holster. She looked relieved. "You had me bothered for a minute, son. I was beginnin' to think you was one of them touchy gents that couldn't take a little good-natured funnin'." She chuckled throatily, remembering. "You got to admit, now,

that it ain't right often that you get to see a feller givin' hisself a top-to-bottom scourin' out in the middle of a horse
pen."

Sharp words to match his mood were on the tip of his
tongue—but he made himself swallow them. Not much
chance of learning anything about Brown if he started
off by turning the citizens against him. "Shade's the name,"
he said pleasantly enough, ignoring all references to the
bathing incident, "Frank Shade. Just landed in Tribulation a
little while ago."

The face was now as bland as a ball of biscuit dough. "I
figured. There ain't many people in these parts that I don't
know." She scratched her head. "And I sure never seen a
face like yours before . . . and that's a fact. What brings
you to Tribulation, Shade? If I ain't gettin too personal."

He hesitated. Was it too soon to start probing? Recalling
the recent bushwhacking attempt, he decided it was not. "I
judge you've lived in Tribulation a while," he said tentatively.

"A while!" There was disbelief in her voice. "Horseblanket Mary rode into town on the first load of rawhide lumber. That's how long I've lived here. I bed down over there
in the end bunk house—in case you been wonderin' what
I'm doin' around the wagon yard."

The woman of the raucous, free and easy laughter had
vanished. Horseblanket Mary, as she called herself, was
suddenly all caution and suspicion. "Why? What makes you
ask?"

"I wasn't pryin', ma'am. Just makin' talk."

She studied him thoughtfully. "You ain't sore about the
funnin'?"

"Like you say, it's a sorry man that can't take a little
hurrahin'."

She was getting more suspicious all the time. If Horseblanket Mary was anything at all, she was a shrewd judge

of human nature. And she could see that here was a man with a very poorly developed sense of humor—he would be a long while forgetting that bathing incident.

Shade cleared his throat and maintained a conversational tone. "Looks like a quiet town you got here. Guess you don't get too many strangers. . . ."

The button eyes glinted. *Ah!* they seemed to say. *So that's it!* And Shade knew that his play acting had been for nothing. He had run up against this kind of stone-headed silence too many times before.

"Good night, Shade," the woman said abruptly. She turned and waddled off into the darkness. A dark, shapeless figure following the circle of the corral fence, making for her own bunk shack.

II

There were no chairs in the shack, no tables, no furniture at all except for the two rope-strung bunks. A coal-oil lamp hung on a wall bracket beside the door. Shade struck a match and held it to the wick until a sputtering, smoky flame danced toward the unceiled roof.

Shade studied the finger-width cracks between the warped boards of the wall. It was easy to imagine that he was a boy again, back in one of a hundred end-of-track shanties of his childhood. He put that thought from his mind.

He sat on his saddle in the corner of the room and carefully dried, cleaned, and oiled his .45.

Pleasant Potter said irritably, "What in damnation you doin'?" He lay on his back with his eyes tightly closed. His right hand still held firmly to his rifle.

"I been talkin' to a woman," Shade said. "Calls herself Horseblanket Mary."

The old man squinted with one eye and snorted. "I know her. And her kind. Gambler, kind of. Deals monte to the Comanches, over at the Injun camp." The one eye opened a little wider. "What did she have to say?"

Shade shook his head. "Nothin'. When I started to ask about strangers in the neighborhood her jaws locked. It always happens wherever Brown is, or has been."

"You still figure Brown's in Tribulation?"

"I'm sure of it. If not actually in the town, he's somewheres close by."

The old man chewed on this for several seconds. Finally he said, "You try offerin' Horseblanket Mary money?"

Shade frowned. "No."

"It's the only thing that'll get her talkin'. And I guess not even *that* would do it—much as Mary likes money—talkin' to a stranger like yourself." He shrugged and closed the one eye. "In the mornin' I'll talk to her. We ain't exactly friends, not by a long shot, but at least she knows me and knows I ain't a lawman."

Shade spent a restless night on the sagging upper bunk.

Tribulation started simmering before the sun was an hour high. Shade and the old man breakfasted on fat dry-salt meat and eggs at a place next to the wagon yard called the Drover's Cafe. The counterman studied them throughout the meal. "Seen you when you rode in last night," he told them at last. "Figure to settle here in Tribulation?"

Shade looked up at the horselike face. "Not if I can help it," he said dryly. But another bushwhacking attempt might make it necessary.

Pleasant Potter spoke without looking up from his plate. "Is Pot Allard still the high muckymuck in these parts?"

The counterman backed off for a moment's thought. "Mr.

Allard still runs his Roman Three over on the Comanche Reservation, if that's what you mean."

"Don't reckon you got any law here in Tribulation, have you?" The cafe operator began to freeze. He was getting that lockjaw look that Shade knew so well. Sopping the last of his egg with a sourdough biscuit, the old scout spoke to Shade. "You got two dollars on you?"

Shade scowled but dug into his bradded watch pocket and brought out two silver dollars. Potter pushed one toward the counterman. "This here's for the meal." He pushed out the other coin. "This here's for you, just because we like the way you fry gamey sowbelly. And because we're naturally friendly cusses and like to talk."

The man gazed greedily at the money. "What kind of talk?"

"Take Pot Allard as a example. You reckon he still totes that old Henry around on his saddle, the way he used to?"

The cafe man was obviously relieved. "Sure. Ever'body knows how Mr. Allard favors a Henry."

"Anybody else in these parts favor Henrys?"

The question was dutifully pondered. "Just Mr. Allard, that I know of. And John Monday that owns the Square Deal Store up the street—but he keeps it hangin' on the wall most of the time. Don't use it much except for pottin' varmits."

"Where's Pot and Monday get their shells?"

"Well, John usually keeps a few boxes in the store. . . ."

The old man got up from the stool and hobbled out of the cafe without another word. Shade followed after him, frowning darkly.

"Why didn't you ask him about Brown?"

The scout shrugged, limping down the dirt walk to the rack where he had left the Appaloosa. "These're pore people around here, and most of them are pretty ignorant, but they ain't informers. Oh, they'll talk for money, if they think they ain't tellin' you nothin'. But they's a point they come to, and they won't go past it. Not even money'll move them."

"I know," Shade said sourly. "What about this Pot Allard?"

The old man leaned against the hitch rack, resting his tender feet. "Well, Pot runs two, three thousand beeves over on the reservation. Big man in these parts. His Roman Three headquarters is down below the Prairie Dog Town Fork somewheres, but he lives mostly in line camps with his riders. Allard ain't a bad man, as cowmen go, and I never pegged him as the kind for backshootin'."

"But he does own a Henry."

"So does the storekeeper, Monday, but that don't mean nothin'. Won't be no trouble to find out where Monday was when we was gettin' ourselves bushwhacked." He squinted up at the hot blue sky. "And we'll find out he was right in that store of his, like always. And Pot Allard's got his hands full ridin' herd on them cows. Don't figure much that he'd travel clean over to the Choctaw Nation ever' now an' again, just to rob one of your trains."

"Just the same, I'd like to talk to Mr. Allard and to anybody else that owns a Henry."

"It's your time, if you want to waste it." The old man grinned through his bristling beard. "Course, there *is* a way of locatin' Brown right quick. We could ride out and set on some lonesome creekbank, in the bright sunlight, and the first gent to kind of sneak up and shoot us in the back, why he'd be the feller we're lookin' for."

Shade was in no mood for humor. "How do I locate Allard?"

"Well, if he ain't in Tribulation, and if he ain't out on the prairie doctorin' a wormy steer, or down in some creek bottom pullin' some cow out of a bog—then more'n likely you'll find him out at the big corral of his. About a mile south there's a wagon track that forks off from the mail road. That takes you back to the reservation and right up to Pot's corral—if he ain't changed things since I was through here last."

"That woman—Horseblanket Mary—you stay here and see what you can find out from her. See if you can find out if any strangers, low on supplies, drifted this way."

"You got four, five dollars you can spare?"

"What for?"

"Like you seen at the cafe, it costs money to ask questions in Tribulation. And monte dealers come higher than biscuit shooters."

Shade muttered something under his breath, but he drew an oilskin wrapper from the back pocket and counted out five greenbacks. "How much," he asked bitterly, "do you figure it'll cost to talk to Allard?"

"More'n money," the old man said mysteriously, "if you go out there and start to ruffin' his fur."

III

Pleasant Potter rode slowly toward the cluster of canvas-covered tepees. " 'Major Elliott,' old Long Hair says, 'take some scouts and find me the enemy.' So the major, he comes to me and says, 'Potter, round up four, five of your best Osages. The general wants a thorough scout upstream.' " The old scout mumbled to himself, "General! He wasn't but a lootenant colonel, but back in the war he had been the Boy General—and Custer never let you forget it. . . ."

And Indian came out of a tepee rubbing his head. "Howdy,

White Dog," the old scout said good naturedly. "You been goin' after them Electric Bitters again?"

The young Kiowa grinned wryly.

"Maybe a little of the hair of the dog's what you need," Dr. Pleasant Potter advised in a professional tone.

The Indian shook his head carefully, holding it with both hands.

"Your grass money all gone?" Potter asked with a note of concern.

The Kiowa nodded, wincing.

The scout dug deep into the folds of his hunting shirt, found a four-bit piece and handed it down to the Indian. He studied White Dog with a kind of long-gone expression, then nudged the Appaloosa and rode on.

"So I rounded up the Osages, and the major got his three companies of cavalry, and we started out to find some Injuns for old Long Hair to kill. Cold? Three days we'd been followin' Custer through a blizzard, and him sayin', 'Bear to the left a little,' or 'Bear to the right a mite,' him still leadin' us with that pocket compass of his. When it stopped snowin' there we was on the north bank of the Canadian, just about where we were headed. *Custer's luck*, they called it. So me and Major Elliott and my Osage boys, we . . ."

Potter interrupted his monologue again to speak to two Comanches that he recognized. "Howdy, Big Wolf, how's that new squaw of yours workin' out? Howdy, Little Hawk, we ain't seen you up at the agency lately. Them Quaker preachers ain't roped you and drug you off to a farm school, have they?"

He spoke to others as the Appaloosa plodded familiarly through a pack of barking dogs. Not long ago they had been enemies fighting tooth and nail for the other's hide. Now Potter sometimes thought the Indians were the only real friends he had left. Take White Dog . . .

"We started upstream," he said, picking up the monologue, "leavin' Long Hair and the wagon train and the
rest of his outfit to cross that ice-clogged river. Well, it
didn't take long for Black Hand and his Osages to pick up
the sign, now that it had stop snowin'. Big Cheyenne war
party—sign was about two days' old. So I rode back and
told Custer, and he was tickled as a banty rooster with a
new set of steel gaffs. 'Potter,' says Long Hair to me, 'you
and Major Elliott follow that pack of murderin' renegades
till dark, then set still and wait for the main column.' He had
it in his head that we'd located a party that had raided up
north two weeks before. I tried to tell him maybe it was the
whole Cheyenne Nation we was up against, not just a party
of young hotbloods. He wouldn't listen. Custer never listened
to nobody but hisself. . . ."

Another voice interrupted the old man's reverie—a voice
as soothing as an ungreased axle. "Getjer money down,
boys! What's the matter with you fellers? Too much easy
livin' got you soft? Afraid to take a chance? Hell, the
reservation ain't blowed away, has it? The grass'll keep grow-
in' and you'll keep gettin' your grass money . . ."

Horseblanket Mary, sitting cross-legged on the ground,
dealt cards to four Comanches on a government-issue blanket.
Pleasant Potter nudged the Appaloosa up to the open flap
of the lodge and peered inside. The woman glanced up,
staring at him with a mixture of pleasure and irritation.

"Pleasant Potter, you old cut-throat! I heered you was up
at Fort Sill livin' the life of the idle rich on your gover'-
ment pension. What brings you out to mix with us pore folks?"

"Business," the scout said shortly, taking a bite of tobacco. "With you."

The woman cackled. "Don't get me to laughin', old man.
It makes my side hurt." Her sharp eyes watched him closely.
"You connected with the Army now?" she asked.

42

"Nope."

"Sorry, Potter, I got all the business I can handle. Me and my Comanche friends is havin' ourselves a little game of monte."

Potter was prepared for this. He dug Shade's crumpled dollar bills out of his pocket and held them for her to see. Mary stared at the bills, then glanced at the small coins in the center of the blanket, and finally she looked at the Indians. "Gents," she said gravely, "it peers like I'm goin' to have to bust up the game for a minute." She put down the cards and reached for the coins, but one of the Indians looked at her and shook his head. "That's right!" she said bitterly. "A pore woman comes out on the short end ever' time, don't she!" She heaved herself up with considerable effort. "I'll be right back, so don't you fellers try to sneak out on me."

Potter rode out a piece from the tepee and waited. Mary waddled toward him, stirring up a small wake of red dust. "Pleasant Potter, if you come out here wastin' my time for . . ."

He showed her the money again. She couldn't make her eyes look away from it. "Talk," he said mildly. "Just a little talk."

She was suspicious. "What about?"

"Well, I'm lookin' for a man. Maybe you can help."

She snorted. "You was always lookin' for some man. A renegade Injun, a ridge rider that had snuck off with the Army payroll, somebody." She sighed, still gazing hungrily at the money. "All right. Who're you after this time?"

"Well," Potter confessed, "I don't exactly know his name, or what he looks like . . ."

Mary threw back her head and cackled again. "Potter, you lost your grip! How do you expect to find somebody when you don't know what he looks like?"

The old man shrugged. "For one thing, this particular gent is mighty partial to a short-barreled scatter-gun." He watched her closely, but mention of Brown's favorite weapon failed to change her expression.

"Plenty folks favor scatter-guns."

"This particular gent," Potter pressed, "also owns a .44 Henry, like this rifle of mine. At least we think he does."

Mary pounced on the vagrant pronoun. "We?"

"My partner," the scout admitted. "The feller you flushed out of the horse trough last night."

The woman grinned. Suddenly the grin vanished and suspicion returned. "This partner of yours, maybe *he's* with the Army?"

Potter shook his head.

"Or maybe a deputy with the U.S. Marshal's office?"

Once again the old scout wagged his head. "You might call it a personal matter with this partner of mine. Me, I'm just in it for the money." He fluttered the bills. "Like you."

She lunged at the money, but Potter jerked it away. "I don't know nothin'," she whined, "about scatter-guns and such."

"Maybe you seen a stranger pass this way the past few days."

"Folks come and go," she said without much hope of ever getting her hands on that money. "Mostly go, here in Tribulation. Anything special about this stranger, except for his scatter-gun and Henry rifle?"

"Well . . ." The scout hesitated, his sharp gaze studying the doughy face. "Might be," he said slowly, "that this here gent's a open-handed kind of cuss. A real do-gooder, especially where money's concerned."

The woman's small eyes grew smaller, sharper, all but disappearing behind folds of grayish flesh. "You're wastin' your time, Potter." She sounded listless. Not even the money seemed to interest her. "There ain't nobody like that in Tribulation." Without as much as a nod, she wheeled and waddled back to the tepee.

Potter sighed and pocketed the money. He found Mary's actions highly interesting. There wasn't much that a woman like Horseblanket Mary wouldn't do for five dollars. But she hadn't even tried to make up a story. It was a curious thing. More than that—it was downright mysterious.

The old scout frowned, puzzled as Mary disappeared into the tepee and dropped the flap. Then he shrugged and reined back toward Tribulation.

"Well," the monologue went on automatically, "sure enough, we found the Cheyennes camped in the bottom next to the river. 'Potter,' says Major Elliott, 'what's it look like down there to you?' 'Major,' I tell him, 'that shore ain't no four-bit raidin' party down there.' They was tepees as far as you could see—which wasn't too far at that, come to think of it. Considerin' the big cloud of lodge smoke that laid over ever'-thing. . . ."

Chief Scout Pleasant Potter was back on the Washita, moving familiarly among the ghosts.

IV

Shade had no way of knowing what it was like at the Allard headquarters down below the Prairie Dog Town Fork of the Red, but up here in Comanche country he hadn't gone in much for trimmings. Just across the reservation boundary he crossed one of the Allard line camps—a half dugout with a sod roof, just big enough for stacked bunks and a small stove. Shade rode toward the hut and called a hello, but

the riders were out taking care of Allard's cattle. No smoke
came from the stovepipe that elbowed out of the shack's one
window.

Shade headed the claybank east and began to see a scattering of cattle in the draws and gullies. The big III brand
was on their sides. The Roman Three.

He topped a grassy rise. No riders were in sight. He
drew his .45 and fired once into the air, then he settled
down to wait.

In a matter of minutes two horsemen topped a shaggy
knoll and pounded across the flatland in Shade's direction.
The lead rider was a big square-jawed man with startlingly
blue eyes set in a weathered face. The blue eyes, when
Shade saw them, were hot with anger. "What the hell's the
matter with you!" he yelled, as soon as he got within shouting distance. "You want to scatter this stock all over the
Territory?"

He didn't know much about cattle and didn't particularly
care whether they scattered or not. "Sorry," he said indifferently. "I was tryin' to raise somebody that could tell me
where to find Pot Allard." He squinted at the big man. "I
don't guess you're Allard, are you?"

"No I ain't," the man said with controlled hostility. "What
do you want to see him about?"

Before answering, Shade briefly studied the second rider.
He was young, slender almost to the point of frailty. He sat
his saddle with arrogance and smiled at Shade. The face
was long and smooth, the mouth delicate and weak, the
eyes pale and hard. Shade learned later, without surprise,
that the man's name was Handsome Corry, a gun specialist
from South Texas hired by Allard to take care of any small
unpleasantness that might arise. The big man was Babe Tattersall, Roman Three foreman.

46

"What do you want with Allard?" Tattersall asked again in the same cold tone.

"Business," Shade evaded.

"I'm the foreman and authorized to take care of any cow business that comes up. You the government contractor from Sill?"

Shade shook his head. "It ain't beef business. It's personal."

Grudgingly, Tattersall nodded to the young gunman. "Ride with him to the Durell place. And stay close to him till you're sure everything's all right."

Handsome Corry shrugged. "Maybe Mr. Allard don't like to be bothered when he's out courtin'."

A subtle change firmed the tough lines of Tattersall's face. Without another word to Shade, the foreman kneed his animal around and rode back in the direction from which he had come.

Shade and Corry, bearing southwest, rode for several minutes in silence. At last Shade said, "Who's Durell?"

Corry glanced at him with those hard, pale eyes and grinned. "I'm Corry—they call me Handsome." He spoke the name proudly, as if it were an honored title that he had earned.

Shade asked again, "Who's Durell?"

Corry appeared to ponder the name. "Whit Durell ain't nothin' at all, I guess. Just a squatter. A sodbuster, like all the rest, workin' and sweatin' on a worthless claim. He'd of starved out long ago I reckon, if it wasn't for that girl of his."

Shade looked at him, frowning. Suddenly Corry laughed. "You wouldn't know Pot Allard if he walked up and spit in your eye, would you?"

Shade saw no point in lying. "I guess I wouldn't."

"And you don't know Bess Durell?"

47

Shade shook his head. "What about her?"

"Wait till you see her. Then you'll know. One time or other half the menfolks in Greer County camped out at Whit Durell's soddy. You ought to of seen them, swarmin' like bees in clover, until . . ." One moment Corry was grinning, the next moment those pale eyes were as cold as winter rain.

Shade studied the young gunman with interest. *Until,* he thought to himself, completing Corry's sentence in his mind . . . *Until Pot Allard, the big cattleman himself, took a shine to the girl?* Is that what Corry had been about to say when caution overtook him?

Shade recalled a shadow of bitterness in Babe Tattersall's eyes when Corry had mentioned courting. Now Corry, for just a moment, allowed the same expression to crack his bland mast. The gunman, with youth, looks, and confidence all on his side, must have been especially put out when the boss himself took a hand in the courting bee and thus, by merely revealing his interest, put an end to all competition.

CHAPTER FOUR

I

WHIT DURELL'S soddy stood near a grove of cottonwoods, beside the bank of a little bitter water stream that twisted down from the crystal capped hills to the west. A small stand

THE GRABHORN BOUNTY

of corn and a slightly larger field of cotton grew in some
cleared bottomland along the creek. A patch for vegetables
had been broken near the house. It seemed to Shade that
Durell's farm talents hadn't made much impression on the
prairie. Weeds were in the corn and cotton, bleeding the
life from the plants. Besides the soddy, there wasn't much to
see in the way of buildings. A rawhide corral, the inevitable
brush arbor, and a frail shed of bleached cottonwood plank-
ing.

As Shade and Corry rode toward the soddy, Shade studied the two men who had been talking together in front of
the shed. Now all talk had stopped. They watched the approaching horsemen.

One man wore the uniform of the prairie sodbuster—bib
overalls, heavy brogans, blue cotton shirt. Shade pegged him
immediately as the farmer, Whit Durell. He was a thin
man in his middle forties, with a grayish look about him
that made him appear much older.

The second man was obviously most of the things the
other was not—tough, ambitious, aggressive, successful. At
first glance he looked like any other saddle-lean, middle-
aged cowhand—but the observer soon caught his mistake.
There was something in the way he stood, with one boot
propped on a wagon tongue, that told Shade that here was
no man to fit a common mold.

Pot Allard and Durell were about the same age, but the
gray in Allard's hair suggested strength of experience. The
cattleman was dressed no better than his foreman and not
so well as Handsome Corry—yet there was an indefinable
something about the man that pointed him out as one who
gave orders. A standard wood-gripped .45 was worn casually, as if it had been a branding iron or some other
piece of everyday equipment. Shade glanced at a brown and
white pinto dozing in front of the soddy, noting the breech

and walnut stock of a fifteen-shot Henry riding in the saddle boot.

Handsome Corry cast long glances toward the dark doorway as he and Shade rode past the soddy. Now Shade saw why. A girl had suddenly appeared in the doorway. Shade's first impression of Bess Durell was one of airy lightness and fragility and extreme youth, although she was probably in her middle twenties. She stepped out of the soddy, her hands hidden in an apron, her eyes wide as she stared at the two riders.

Corry flashed a grin at the girl. She appeared not to see it. Her eyes grew wider as she methodically noted every small detail of Shade's rig and appearance. Even after they had passed the soddy, putting the girl behind them, Shade found that he could close his eyes for a moment and still see the wide-eyed, childlike face of Bess Durell. The experience startled him, and he twisted in the saddle to look back at her.

He was beginning to understand Corry's words when they had first started riding in this direction. *Wait till you see her*, the gunman had said. *Then you'll know.*

Well, Shade thought warily, he had to admit there was something about this girl that affected men in unusual ways.

They reined up in front of the farm wagon. Shade, with an effort, blocked Bess Durell from his mind and looked at the cattleman.

"Mr. Allard?"

Allard fixed a bulletlike gaze on Shade's face. "I take it you're the gent that's been askin' about me over at Tribulation."

For the second time in as many minutes Shade was startled. News traveled fast on the prairie.

Allard moved his gaze to Handsome Corry. "Me and Babe Tattersall come across him over by the west camp," the

gunman explained. "Babe says show him over here. So I
did."

Allard nodded. "Your job's to see that rustlers and Indians don't steal me blind, not to conduct guided tours of
the reservation. You remind Tattersall of that when you see
him. Now get back to your work."

A spot of color appeared in Corry's cheeks. For just a
moment he gazed at his boss in that certain unblinking, unmistakable way peculiar to poisonous snakes and other
killers. Then he ducked his head and pulled his hat down
over his eyes. "Whatever you say, Mr. Allard." Abruptly
he reined back toward the reservation.

Allard's direct gaze was back on Shade's face. "All right,"
he said coldly, "you've just cost me the services of a good
hand for half a day. That half a day could cost me a half
a hundred head of beef, if rustlers happen to know about it.
Which," he added, with a touch of Corry's own deadliness,
"I hope, for your sake, will not be the case."

Shade preferred to overlook the threat. "Can we talk in
private, Mr. Allard?"

"This is private enough for me." Just the same, he did
glance at Durell.

The farmer shrugged. "There's some things I ought to
be doin', anyhow." He glanced thoughtfully and a little fear-
fully at the stranger on the claybank gelding. "I'll be over
at the soddy, Mr. Allard, if there's anything you want . . ."

When they were alone, Shade climbed down from the
saddle, grounded the reins and methodically built himself a
smoke. "My name's Shade," he said. "I work for the Choctaw and Canadian Valley Railroad over in the Nations. You'll
notice I'm a long way from home ground—but, then, so is
the man I'm lookin' for."

Allard said nothing. Shade selected a match from his hat-
band and lit his smoke. "I'm tellin' you this because I've

got the feelin' you know about it already. You knowed about me landin' in Tribulation fast enough."

"I also know you was travelin' with an old Army squaw man called Pleasant Potter," Allard said bluntly. "Potter and me ain't exactly friends. More'n once, when I go to lease reservation grass, he's gone to the Indians and gets them to run up the price. Unofficially, of course, out of the hands of the agents. But I have to meet the higher price or stand to lose even more beef than I do to rustlers—if you know what I mean."

Shade nodded to indicate that he understood. Potter's little game of blackmail didn't surprise him. Clearly, the old scout held Indians superior to white intruders; he had never made any bones about that.

"It's my nature," Allard continued, "to mistrust you or anybody else that rides with Potter. You better say what you come to say, so we can get this over with."

"That's fine with me. I'll start by askin' how you knowed I worked for the railroad?"

Allard's look had the smooth blankness of glass. He had no intentions of answering the question.

"Well," Shade went on, "maybe you can tell me when was the last time you fired that Henry. The one over there in your saddle boot."

The cattleman's eyes were mere slits. "Why?"

"Call it personal reasons. Of course, if you don't want to answer . . ."

"I don't mind," Allard said. Shade's forehead wrinkled. Was it imagination, or had the rancher's willingness to cooperate come a little too suddenly? "I shot a coyote with that Henry," the rancher said off-handedly, "just this mornin'."

"You had a chance to clean it yet?"

There was an instant's hesitation. ". . . No, not yet."

"Mind if I have a look at the rifle?"

The questions were too pointed for Allard's liking, but for the moment he held his temper. "Maybe you wouldn't mind answerin' a question for me, Shade. What's so interestin' about that rifle of mine?"

Shade grinned, but it was a brittle, humorless expression, and Pot Allard understood it thoroughly. "Yesterday around sundown a rifle just like yours nigh took my head right off my shoulders. So I take more'n common interest anytime I see a Henry."

Now Allard loosened the rein on his temper. "I don't take kindly to bein' called a bushwhacker, Shade. Unless you can show some proof, you better start backin' some water."

Shade pretended not to hear. "I didn't mention bushwhack," he said mildly. "How'd you know that's what it was?"

"If it wasn't bushwhack, you'd *know* who'd nearly shot you, instead of makin' accusations to everybody that happens to be carryin' a Henry." He smiled a smile to match Shade's own. "I ain't partial to bushwhackers, myself. I understand how a thing like that could get you to boil over and say things you don't mean. Which," he added for emphasis, "is the only reason I ain't takin' this as personal as I might . . ."

But Shade, bent on going his own direction, broke in. "It didn't happen far from here. North a little from that line camp of yours—so it was probably on your range."

"I don't know anything about the shootin'," Allard said grimly.

"Then you won't mind if I just take a look at that rifle."

The cattleman flushed. He wasn't used to being pushed. "Reach for that Henry," he said huskily, "and it'll be the last move you'll ever make." With visible effort he took control of his anger. "Get on your animal, Shade. Go back to work for the railroad; we've got nothin' else to talk about."

From where Shade stood he could not see the soddy, but

he had the uneasy feeling of a man whose every move is being watched over the sights of a gun. He breathed deeply, decided that suicide was the answer to nothing, and reached for the claybank's reins.

"Just a minute," Allard said. "Maybe there's somethin' you ought to see before you go." With a nod he indicated a tree standing near the grove of cottonwoods. "See that pecan tree?"

Shade glanced at the tall tree with its clusters of green hulled nuts. "What about it?"

"The top fork," the cowman said. "The branch that bends over to the north."

Scowling, Shade located the branch. "I still say what about it?"

Allard turned slowly to face the tree. Then, in a casual way he reached for his .45, took an instant to aim, and fired. The top of the pecan tree shuddered. The branch in question separated from its parent limb and floated lazily to the ground.

"I just wanted you to know," Allard said, turning and holstering the revolver, "that if I had been the bushwhacker, you wouldn't be in any shape today to complain."

Shade faced the rancher with a sour grin. "The thing is, I ain't exactly sure the bushwhacker was aimin' to kill. Maybe he figured to burn a couple past my head and scare me off the trail—that would take pretty good shootin' too."

Allard's expression went blank. "Believe what you like, but I don't want to see you on the Roman Three again. And I wouldn't like to hear of you botherin' the Durells, either."

"I never was one to force hisself on folks," Shade said dryly. "But I haven't said yet what it was that brought me here, or why it was that somebody might want to kill me."

"I don't mix in other folks' business," Allard said shortly, "and I don't like them mixin' in mine."

Shade could feel the ice getting thin. Better to ride out now, while he was still able, and think over what he had learned. He nodded to the cowman in mock politeness and reined the claybank west. As he rode past the soddy he caught the glint of gunsteel in the open window as Whit Durell quickly put the weapon out of sight. Against the gloom of the soddy's interior, Shade could not tell what type of weapon it was. "I'd give a pretty," he said aloud, "to know if it was a sawed-off scatter-gun."

Bess Durell stood in the doorway watching Shade with those wide eyes. In this harsh, monotonous country of little beauty, any breath of femininity was as welcome as rain. But this girl was something more than the usual run of prairie womanhood. In this flat country her quiet beauty was as spectacular as a sunset.

Shade touched his hatbrim as he rode past. Her expression did not change. Shade continued to sēē her in his mind long after the soddy was out of sight.

II

Pleasant Potter sat on the dirt walk in front of the Texas Bar, his back to a fire barrel, his eyes closed. His only sign of consciousness was the monotonous working of his whiskered jaws on the inevitable cud of tobacco. He heard the Appaloosa switching flies at the hitch rack, only a few feet away, and he heard a dog barking in the distance. All day long he had been talking to folks that he had known for years. But today they had been strangers.

It was a curious thing. The old scout had given it no little thought, but as yet had arrived at no satisfactory con-

clusion. He had talked to people, sized them up with his
eyes, and now he was studying them with his ears.

To the casual listener there would have been much to
hear—but silence itself had something to tell an experienced
scout. Silence could say as much as a scream, if you knew
how to listen.

From across the alley to the west came the rapid swish-
ing of a corn broom. It was a nervous sound. That would
be John Monday, the Square Deal owner, sweeping out his
general store. Monday was a nervous man. This was the
second time he had swept out since Potter had been sitting
there on the walk. "And places just don't get that dirty," the
old man thought dryly. "Not even in Tribulation."

The Texas Bar was without customers, but Potter could
hear the barkeep, Tom Murdles, pacing back and forth in
front of the door. For some reason Murdles felt that he had
to keep an eye on Potter.

"Yes sir," the old man said placidly to himself, "she's a
nervous town, all right. Puts me in mind of the major when
he got his first squint at that bunch of Cheyenne lodges . . ."
The back of Potter's mind drifted in the past, but the front,
the conscious part, still listened to the town. " 'Lord knows
how many lodges we'll find on down the river,' the major
says. 'For all we know there could be Arapaho and Apache
camps, as well as Cheyenne. There might even be some
Comanches, though I guess that ain't likely. We'll never
I guess, until we look.' 'Major,' I says, 'it really don't make
a damn's worth of difference how many Injuns is down there
in that bottom. Old Long Hair, he's already got it figured
it's just that raidin' party of Cheyenne, and he won't listen
to nothin' else. You know how *he* is when . . .' "

From the east Potter heard the solid clop of hoofs and recognized the sound of Shade's claybank gelding. He squinted
with one eye, watching the rider circle the cluster of Com-

manche lodges and head toward the wagon yard. "So the major says, 'Call in your Osages, Potter. We'll scout downstream a ways and report back to the gen'ral. . . .'" With a grunt, the old scout lurched up from the dirt walk and hobbled to the Appaloosa. With considerable effort and a good deal of profanity he pulled himself up to the saddle and reined east to meet Shade. The Battle of the Washita was left hanging.

They met at the bunk shack after Shade had paid Ludlow Finch for another night's rent. "Guess you and Pot Allard hit it off all right," the old man observed. "You got back with no extry holes in your hide, looks like."

"No thanks to you," Shade grunted. "Why didn't you tell me he was an expert shot?" The old man shrugged. "Don't hurt yourself laughin'," Shade told him spitefully. "You ain't exactly a pal of his, you know."

"I reckon not. On account of me, he had to pay a halfway fair price for his Injun grass. What you aim to do now?"

"Wash up and put somethin' in my belly."

Pleasant Potter crossed his arms on the saddle horn and slouched forward on the Appaloosa. "Never could trust a man that washes all the time," he grumbled. He thought about getting down, but he hated the thought of touching the ground with his tender feet, so he kept his seat on the Indian pony while Shade went to the pump and took off the top layer of dust.

"Well," the old man asked blandly when Shade had returned from the pump, "was it Pot Allard that tried to shoot us out of our saddles yesterday?"

Shade took his time answering. ". . . I ain't decided. But if it was him, he was shootin' to scare, not to kill."

The old man listened while Shade reviewed the day for him. "So Pot's got him a gunhand now," he commented

57

with a thoughtful spat at the ground. "Nothin' very queer about that, though. Most cowmen on the reservation put one, maybe more, on the payroll to give the rustlers somethin' to think about." He squinted into the distance. "What did you say the name of that squatter was?"

"Whit Durell."

Potter shook his head. "Don't recollect the name. Must be a newcomer. And folks in Tribulation don't talk much about newcomers—that's only thing I found out today."

"Allard already knew all about us bein' in Tribulation and askin' questions. It struck me that he knew a little too much about us, even if he *is* a big cowman that people go out of their way to tell things to."

But the old scout's thoughts had branched off in another direction. "This squatter gal—she must be a lot of gal to corral an old brush bull like Allard."

"She's that, all right," Shade said in a strange tone. "Handsome Corry claimed most of the male population in these parts had camped in the Durell dooryard before Allard took an interest and scared them off." Shade stuffed in his shirt, combed his black hair with his fingers and started toward the Drover's Cafe. Potter followed alongside on the Appaloosa. "What did you find out in town?"

The old man glared disgustedly at the listless town. "Never heard a word about Brown, or a do-gooder, or a shot-gunner, or anything else, for that matter, except . . ." He scratched a bewhiskered jaw. "When somebody like Horseblanket Mary, with the gall of a bull buffalo, locks her jaws in the face of cash money, then you can bet folks is scared."

Shade scowled. "What about the storekeeper with the Henry?"

The scout shrugged. "He runs the Square Deal by hisself,

so he couldn't of very well knocked off work for a little bush-whackin' without somebody noticin' it, but he does carry Henry shells in his store."

They paused in front of the drab cafe. Shade was again feeling the weight of defeat. Fear and suspicion were in the town, but Brown's familiar pattern was missing. "There was one thing I had counted on," he told Potter, "to point Brown out to me once I had tracked him into a corner. That pattern of his of locatin' people that need help in the worst way, and then helpin' them with money that he stole from the Grabhorns. You wouldn't think that loyalty would be a thing you could buy with cold cash, would you? But I guess it is, if you go about it right. Anyhow, it's the way Brown always worked before—he could always count on folks to hide him out, long as his do-good money held out."

"Maybe he's run out of money."

Shade grinned sourly. "It ain't likely." He shook his head. "The pattern just ain't here. I'm afraid we made a long ride for nothin'."

"Well," the old man drawled, "if this *does* turn out to be a snipe hunt, and if the feller that led us to Tribulation *ain't* Brown, then I'd be mighty interested to know just who it was that tried to drygulch us yesterday."

It always came back to that bushwhacking. Shade looked at the old man with a grudging grin. Pleasant Potter stood to earn his cut of the Grabhorn bounty, after all—even if he did nothing but keep Shade on the right track.

III

It was the usual thing to find one or two Roman Three horses at the hitchrack in front of the saloon—there was one there now. And a Roman Three wagon was loading feed at the Square Deal.

Shade was washing down a bad supper with worse whiskey at the Texas Bar. Pleasant Potter sat at a card table, resting his tender feet, with a bottle of his own. Near the end of the plank bar an Allard cowhand was idly punching colored balls around a battered pool table.

"What time is it?" the cowhand asked without looking up from the faded green felt.

"Eight o'clock," Tom Murdles, the barkeep said, consulting his nickel-plated timepiece.

"Then bring me another whiskey."

The barkeep poured the drink and set it on the edge of the pool table, and the cowhand continued banking the balls.

It was a dreary night, Shade was thinking, in a dead town full of frightened people. He glanced at the old man, but Potter was staring into his glass, mumbling to himself. Fighting the Battle of the Washita again, no doubt. Shade turned his attention to Tom Murdles, a mild little man, completely bald except for a fringe of reddish hair around his ears. On two occasions Shade had tried to strike up a conversation, and both times Murdles had found things to do in the rear of the saloon.

Through the open door Shade could see the glowing cones of Comanche tents. But Tribulation, except for the saloon and general store, was dark. Shade moved to the old man's table.

Potter looked up, bringing Shade slowly into focus. "Patience," he said dryly. "You got to learn to let a thing simmer. If Brown's here he'll let it be known, sooner or later. They's a limit to how many questions a feller like that can stand for."

"What good's askin' questions if there ain't any answers?"

"Maybe no good at all." The old man poured himself one more drink and corked the bottle. "But it'll be hard for Brown to know for sure whether we're gettin' answers or whether we ain't. Before long he'll start gettin' nervous, and when a feller gets nervous he starts makin' mistakes."

Shade looked up and was startled to see a masklike Indian face staring at him from the darkness of the street. "Potter, I think one of your Comanche pals has come callin'."

The scout turned and squinted. "Ain't Comanche," he said. "Kiowa." He pushed himself up from the table and hobbled toward the door. Shade paid the bartender and followed the old man outside.

"Howdy, White Dog," Potter said amiably. "What brings you off from camp this time o' night?"

The Indian's masklike expression did not change. He spoke for several seconds in guttural Kiowa. Frowning and grunting, the old man listened closely. He spoke briefly in Kiowa, then clapped his friend on the shoulder. "Get back to camp, White Dog. Me and my pard'll come down for a look-see."

The young Kiowa pulled his trade blanket around his brown shoulders. He backed off a few steps and then, ghostlike, disappeared in the night. "What was that all about?" Shade demanded.

The old man limped toward his Appaloosa. "Better get your claybank saddled. They's been some trouble down at the Injun camp. Some white man tried to kill Horseblanket Mary."

IV

White Dog met them in front of the gambling lodge. With considerable gesturing and waving of arms as Kiowas like to do, the Indian told the story as he knew it. Mary had been in the tent dealing monte to several Comanches when the white man had called to her from the darkness. Complaining and grumbling, Mary had interrupted the game to see what the man wanted. The Comanches had heard loud talk between the two, then the woman had cried out, as if in pain. After a short while the commotion ended and the man rode off to the east.

They found Horseblanket Mary laid out on a scabby buffalo robe inside the gambling lodge. There were cuts and bruises on her face. Her mouth was bloody and two front teeth were missing.

"Water," Pleasant Potter said over his shoulder. White Dog disappeared and returned almost immediately with water in a canvas bucket. Potter dribbled some of the water in Mary's mouth and sprinkled the rest of her face. She regained consciousness in a great stir of profanity.

"What're *you* doin' here!" she demanded angrily to Potter as soon as she could speak.

"White Dog caught me at the saloon and said you'd caught the short end of a misunderstandin'. How bad are you hurt?"

The woman felt of her fat ribs, grimacing. "Ain't nothin' broke, I guess." She dabbed at her puffy mouth. "Except some teeth, seems like." Panting heavily, she managed to raise herself to her elbows. Shade knelt and started to give her a hand, but she drew back and snarled, "Stay away from me! Just go away from here and leave me alone!" She glared at the old man. "You too, Potter! This never would of happened if it hadn't been for you!"

Potter and Shade glanced at each other. "Who was it done this, Mary?" the old man asked softly.

"None o' your damn business, old man! Just get away from me, like I say!"

Gathering her strength, she tried mightily to lift herself to a sitting position. Her face twisted and turned white. She gasped and settled back on the shaggy robe. "Reckon I ain't in such good shape after all. Rib or two got busted, feels like."

"Lay where you are," Shade told her. "I'll ride back and rustle up a doctor."

She stared at him with those black button eyes. Abruptly she laughed, but the sound turned to coughing and gasping.

"The closest doctor's down below the Prairie Dog Town Fork at Henrietta—that's maybe forty, fifty miles," the old man said. "There might be a Army doc up at Sill, but I don't know how you'd get him down here to Tribulation."

"I don't need a doc," Mary said angrily. "You think this is the *first* time I ever had busted ribs?" She closed her eyes tightly. "Just get away from me! Leave me alone!"

The monte-playing Comanches had long since cleared out of the lodge, but now a curious crowd of Indians peered cautiously through the open flap. Shade nodded to the old man. "Ask your friends if they know anything about this. Somebody must of seen somethin' out there."

"I'll try," Potter grumbled, "but it won't do any good. Pore Lo's grabbed hold of the short end of the stick too many times before. He's learned it don't pay to mix in white man's doin's." He stepped out of the lamplighted tepee and spoke to the crowd in Comanche, the one language that all plains

Indians understood. He didn't even get a grunt in answer
to his questions. One by one the Indians melted away. Even
White Dog had slipped away in the darkness.

Potter ducked back into the tepee shaking his head. "They
got trouble enough of their own, they don't want to borrow
none of ours."

Shade stood silent, scowling, trying to decide on the best
road to take. He felt responsible—and knew that he was
responsible—for what had happened to Horseblanket Mary.
Somebody, fearing that sooner or later she might give in to
temptation and tell what she knew, had offered this beating
as a warning.

In a way this was good news to Shade. Somebody knew
exactly what had brought him to Tribulation, and the knowledge made that somebody very nervous. It meant that Shade
was, at last, on the right track.

He looked at Potter. "We can't just leave her here, can
we?"

"Well . . ." The old scout chewed thoughtfully. "I don't
reckon the Injuns'll bother her. Long's she's here they won't
come no closer to this tepee than they would a smallpox tent."

"Wouldn't do to jostle her around," Shade thought out
loud. "We could rustle up some grub, and some medicine,
maybe, if the store's still open."

The old man nodded noncommittally while Mary glared
up at them, her face growing redder and redder. "Can't
neither one of you fools understand a word I tell you?
I don't never want to look at you again! That's *all* I want!"

Shade moved his shoulders and sighed. "I don't guess
you'd be interested in tellin' us who the man was, or why
he gave you this beatin'."

She tried to sneer but her puffy lips wouldn't curl. "Didn't
nobody give me a beatin'. I stumped my toe on a wagon
tongue—it was a accident."

"The next accident could be fatal," Shade told her.

"They won't *be* a next one, if you and that old fool will clear out and let me be!"

She was a tough one. Likely there wasn't much in the way of devilment that she hadn't tried in her time. But now she was an old woman, and helpless, and scared. Shade knew from experience that talking would only be a waste of time.

The two men left the gambling lodge, mounted and headed back to Tribulation. The street was deserted. The Roman Three wagon was gone. And so was the cowhand. The bartender was just locking the door to the Texas Bar as the two riders reined up at the rack.

"Just a minute," Shade said. "I want a bottle of whiskey before you close up."

The mild little barkeep shot furtive glances up and down the street. "I . . . I'm sorry, gents, the place is already locked."

With an abruptness that surprised even himself, Shade found that he had run out of patience. "Unlock it," he said harshly, swinging down from the saddle, "if you don't want your door shot off its hinges."

Pleasant Potter sat his Appaloosa, grinning in dim amusement. It looked like the railroader was beginning to get riled. In his naturally curious mind, the scout had wondered several times how this big homely galoot would react once he was prodded to a fighting temper.

The barkeep had no such curiosity. Quickly he unlocked the door, the key rattling in his nervous hand. Shade stepped inside and lighted the bracket lamp near the door. "Make it two bottles," he said. Mary struck him as a woman who could work up a handsome thirst.

Pleasant Potter, reluctant to punish his tender feet, remained in the saddle. He was curiously observing a stir of activity inside the Square Deal, across the alley from the saloon, when Shade came out of the Texas Bar. Shade stuffed the whiskey in his saddlebags. Then, for a moment, he stood in the street watching Tom Murdles hurriedly blowing out his coal-oil lamps.

"Peers like folks ain't very anxious to get our business," the old scout observed mildly.

Bad news traveled fast. The tall stranger and the old man were poison in Tribulation. The less the citizens could have to do with them, the better they liked it. Shade climbed the front loading ramp and grabbed the Square Deal's door before Monday could close it.

"I know it's past closin' time," Shade said dryly, "and you was just lockin' up, but I got a grocery order I want filled anyhow." And there was something about the eyes a certain stubborn jutting of the chin, that advised caution. Monday hesitated, then backed away, leaving one lamp burning on the front counter. "Mr. Shade . . ." He had to clear his throat. "If you could come back tomorrow . . ."

"Tonight," Shade said softly. "Tonight and right now."

Neither tone nor word left any margin for further delay. Swallowing hard, the storekeeper moved behind the counter. "Two pounds of crackers," Shade told him. "A pound of that cheese. Two cans of them stewed tomatoes, and a can of peaches. Two cans of sardines and one can of salmon."

Monday scurried from shelf to shelf getting the order together. "And throw in a dozen of them jawbreakers," Shade said. The hard candy would be something for the old woman to hold in her mouth in the absence of teeth. "And a bar of tar soap and some sulphur ointment."

Monday was out of ointment. He dumped the other things in a spare sugar sack and made out the bill. "Mr. Shade," he said stiffly, taking his pay, "if it's the same to you, I'd as soon you took your business some place else after this."

Shade grinned toothily. "I bet." It was then that he noted

the gleam of gunsteel on the far wall. He stepped over and took the Henry down from its rack before the storekeeper had a chance to object. Sniffing at the breech and the muzzle, he could detect nothing but gun oil and steel. "How long's it been since you shot this gun?"

"Now look here!" Monday blustered. Then, once again, he noted that certain glint in the tall man's eyes and went on in a quieter tone. "I shot a coyote this mornin', if that's any of your business."

Shade replaced the rifle. The Henry had been cleaned within the past few hours. If it was the bushwhack gun, there was no way of proving it now.

"You and John hit it off all right?" Pleasant Potter asked as Shade tied the grub sack to his saddle horn.

"Mr. Monday was the soul of cooperation," Shade muttered. "But he didn't have any healin' salve. I think there's some in my warbag, over at the camp shack."

They reined toward the wagon yard.

A square of white paper fluttered on the door of their shack. Shade looked at it and a certain feeling came over him—a certain tightness of the gut that warns you that the ice you're standing on is starting to crack. He climbed down and jerked the paper off the tack that held it to the door. "Strike a match," he told the old man.

Obligingly, the old man struck a match on his thumbnail and cupped the small flame in his hands. Shade brought the paper close to the flame and read, *GET OUT OF TRIBULATION NOW OR YOULL GET WORSN MARY.*

The note was on ruled tablet paper, the all-purpose stationery of the plains. From the look of it, the message had been printed with a lead bullet.

CHAPTER FIVE

I

ALL THE TEPEES were dark except the gambling lodge. The Indian had a sensitive nose for trouble, and he could smell it now clinging like musk to the two white men and the monte woman. Shade and Potter sat their saddles for a moment in front of the gambling tent. The old scout cocked his head houndlike—almost as though he had caught the scent himself.

They could hear Mary swearing and groaning weakly. Shade climbed down and took the grub sack and whiskey into the tent. The old man nudged his Appaloosa up to the open flap but did not dismount.

Pain had turned the woman wolfish. "I thought I told you to leave me be!" she snarled.

Shade dropped the grub sack on the buffalo robe, uncorked one of the bottles and handed it to Mary. "This is the best we could do, seein' there's no doctor around. There's grub in the sack, and two quarts of painkiller."

Mary swigged greedily from the neck of the bottle. "I don't need your grub," she hissed, "nor your whiskey neither . . . But I might as well drink it," she added, "seein' as how it's here." She raised the bottle and gulped steadily until it was a quarter empty. "How many times I got to tell you to get away from me?"

"Who gave you this beatin', Mary?"

She sighed wearily. "It's like talkin' to the deaf. Can't you get it through your head that you're goin' to get me killed with these fool questions of yours!"

"What're you afraid of, Mary? What's this whole town afraid of?"

She snatched another swig from the bottle, then stubbornly locked her jaws. "It's all tied up with a man named Brown, ain't it?"

"I don't know no Brown."

Sometimes it was easy for Shade to forget that "Brown" was merely a name of convenience. His real name might be Jones, or Botkin, or Smith, or even Allard. "I work for the Choctaw and Canadian Valley Railroad, Mary." That was no secret. Allard, for one, already knew about it. "I'm lookin' for a man that specializes in robbin' Grabhorn Express cars. He favors shotguns and, maybe, Henry rifles."

The woman snorted and stared glassily at the bottle. "There ain't a railroad in fifty, sixty miles of here.

"When he ain't workin' at the robbin' trade he ain't much for hangin' around railroads," Shade said dryly. "There's somethin' else about this man. He's a do-gooder. Gives his money away like it was nothin', to folks that's down and out. Anybody like that settle around Tribulation lately?"

The whiskey was taking hold. Mary stared blearily at Shade, started to laugh then winced in pain. "There ain't nobody like that in these parts, and that's the truth. Now let me be."

Shade didn't expect direct answers to his questions; the woman was too frightened for that. He had hoped that her reactions, a look or a gesture, might give him something

to go on. Shade was about to give it up as a bad job when
Potter spoke up from the open flap.

"What about folks that lives around here, Mary? Especially them that kind of strays off and gets theirselves lost
for two, three weeks at a time. Maybe longer."

"What you fools take me for! A census taker that goes
around stickin' my nose in other folks' business?" She wanted
to sound indignant, but it came out straight fear.

This, Shade decided, was the time to use his most powerful persuader. "Mary," he said, "there's ten thousand dollars
ridin' on this man's head. A cut of it's yours if you can help
us catch him."

Those dark button eyes stared at his face. "Mister," she
said in a tone of absolute finality, "I like money well's the
next one. But bein' the richest woman in the graveyard
don't exactly suit my fancy. I don't know nothin', and I
ain't sayin' nothin', and that's that."

A door that might have opened onto light had slammed
shut.

Shade left the gambling lodge, mounted the claybank and
rode back toward the wagon yard with the old man. Well,
he thought grimly, as Mary had said, that was that. When a
monte dealer couldn't be tempted with money there was no
use trying it on anybody else.

"What do you make of it?" he asked Potter. "Could Brown
be one of the good citizens of Tribulation? Is that the reason
everybody gets lockjaw every time you start to look curious?"

"Peers that way, don't it?" the old man said mildly.

"I keep thinkin' about Allard. You know him better'n I
do. Could he be the one?"

"I been thinkin' about that. I guess it could be. But if
Pot Allard is Brown, I'd be mighty interested to know why
he took up robbin' when he's gettin' rich and fat just feedin'
his cows on Injun grass."

That thought had crossed Shade's mind too. The rest of the trip to the wagon yard was made in silence.

Surprisingly, Ludlow Finch, the stableman, was waiting for them at the corral when they rode up. Beside the stableman was a good-sized mound of plunder that Shade recognized as his personal belongings and pack gear.

Long frustration opened a door to Shade's anger. He leaned over the claybank's neck and said with a mildness that deceived no one, "If it ain't too much bother, Mr. Finch, maybe you wouldn't mind tellin' us the meanin' of this."

The stableman took a nervous but determined stance. "I cleared out your shack. You fellers can't stay here tonight, or any other night."

"Why?" Shade asked quietly.

"Don't matter why. This wagon yard belongs to me and I can say who can stay here and who can't—and I'm sayin' you fellers can't."

"I've already paid our rent for tonight."

"You can have your money back. But you'll have to find another place." He hesitated briefly. "If it was *me* in your place," he blurted, "I'd clear out of these parts for good! That's what *I'd* do!"

"More'n likely," Shade told him in the same even tone, "but you ain't me. The rent's been paid and I aim to stay out the night in that shack, whether you like it or not, Mr. Finch." He glanced at the old man. "Go on to the shack and bed down. I'll bring the plunder and turn the animals into the corral."

Potter had watched and listened to the exchange with elaborate indifference. Now he shrugged and spat and rode on toward the shack.

"I tell you I won't allow it!" Finch said in a rising voice.

Shade bent farther over the claybank's neck. "Mister, this

has been a disappointin day for me all around I'm beginnin' to get a bellyful of folks tellin' me where to head in " He
kneed his horse forward.

II

Shade stretched his long frame on the hot top bunk but
could not make himself relax. "Potter, you asleep?"

The old man grunted. "Not now, I ain't."

The lamp had been blown out for several minutes but the
stale scent of oil smoke and burnt wick still clung to the
still air. "I thought I heard somethin' movin' out there."

The old scout listened. He had complete confidence in
his hearing. They used to say at Fort Sill that Pleasant Potter
could hear an eagle leaving its nest over in the Ouachitas.
It would never occur to him that Shade could have detected
a sound that he had missed.

"I didn't hear nothin'. Best we get some sleep."

". . . I guess " Maybe, Shade thought, I'm workin' up a
case of nerves. Finch was a nobody. And nobodies never
did anything, they just sat and sweated and fumed and
did nothing. But Finch was a scared nobody, and sometimes
they would fool you.

"Potter, I've got a feelin' about this . . ."

"I thought you was asleep," the old man said with a note
of irritation.

"I ain't asleep. I'm gettin' the feelin' that one of us ought
to be standin' some kind of watch."

Pleasant Potter groaned and said nothing. Shade lay for
several minutes trying to decide whether he ought to get up
and stand watch himself. While he was in the process of

making up his mind, the first of fifteen hard-nosed rifle slugs began to shoot the flimsy shack to pieces.

The shots came fast, crowded one on top of the other with an almost monotonous precision. After it was over a great many thoughts, most of them violent, burned in Shade's brain. But at the time his mind was blank. For one of the few times in his life Shade tasted the gall of panic. While the heavy slugs ripped and splintered the walls of the shack, he lay like a stone man on the top bunk, unable to move, unable even to yell. He could only grip the frame of the bunk, grip until his arms went numb, growing a little colder, a little stiffer, with every leaden slug that struck and smashed the cottonwood walls.

A bullet crashed a corner pole of the double bunk and one corner of Shade's bunk dropped like stone. He could hear the soft timber give way and knew that in a matter of seconds he would be crashing down on top of the old man. He still couldn't make himself move. He couldn't make his hands turn loose of the frame.

In Shade's ears the sound of firing was a constant, thunderous rattle of explosive hailstones. It was impossible to pinpoint the source of the murderous racket. The air inside the shack was clogged with dust and pulpwood splinters. The shack began to collapse. Another supporting timber of Shade's bunk gave way, and everything seemed to go at once.

The bunk crashed to the floor, narrowly missing the old man on the bunk below. The front wall of the camp shack bowed inward. Some of the powder-dry planks cracked. Part of the wall fell in, showering more wood fragments and dust in Shade's face. After a while it occurred to Shade that the shooting had stopped.

At first he had trouble believing it, but it was true. The town was as dead quiet as an abandoned graveyard. The walls of the camp shuddered, and creaked and swayed a little, but the structure did not collapse completely. That moment of silence was as shocking as the thunder of gunfire had been.

Shade stared at a place where, a moment ago, there had been a wall, and saw great patches of night sky and prairie. It was hard to believe that one rifle could have caused so much damage. It was also hard for Shade to believe that he had somehow come through it alive.

He made himself turn loose of the splintered bunk. Instinctively, he felt of himself. Nothing seemed to be broken. The swarm of bullets had somehow passed through the shack without touching him.

Now the moment of panic left him and rage rushed in to take its place. He lurched up from the floor of the shack, fumbling for his revolver. Already the rifleman was getting away. Shade grabbed for the door, which was sagging crazily on one hinge. The bushwhacker was vanishing into the night. The sound of hoofs trailed off to the south, or the east. Before Shade could reach the door, silence had settled again on Tribulation. Then, and not till then, did Shade think about the old man.

"Potter?" He hesitated at the sagging door. "Potter, you all right?"

The old man stirred beneath the litter.

The sound of hoofbeats faded until it was no sound at all. The bushwhacker was getting away clean, as he had gotten away the first time. Strangely, Shade's sense of blind rage was also vanishing. He said again, "Potter, you all right?"

"I ain't . . . right sure . . ." The old man made a sound like a long-drawn-out sigh.

Shade returned to the old man's bunk, quickly brushed away the litter and struck a match. In the harsh light of burning sulphur the old man's face was dead white, colorless. In the light of day it would have been yellowish, the color of death. There was still the breath of life somewhere in that frail old body, but the look of the face was something that Shade had seen too many times before. The taut muscles around the mouth, the set features, the glazed eyes.

Shade moved the flickering match, glimpsed the two spreading spots of crimson on the old man's hunting shirt. The match went out and Shade didn't bother to light another.

Potter was beginning to feel his wounds. After a while he spoke in that sighing voice. "Give my plunder to White Dog. He ain't a bad Injun—for a Kiowa."

"You ain't checkin' in yet, old man. I'll go over to Monday's store and see what I can find in the way of medicine."

Potter gestured limply. "Medicine won't help. . . ." For a moment his mind wandered, skirting the edges of a dark, strange country. Perhaps he was back on the Washita with Custer and Elliott and the others. Shade heard him grunt involuntarily as the pain grew hotter.

"Potter . . ." A sensation of hollowness was growing in Shade's gut. "Potter, is there anything I can do?"

The old man dwelled on this for several seconds. "They's plenty worse ways to check in," he said at last, in a voice that was barely a shadow of a whisper.

"Potter, is there anything you want?"

"Well now," the old man breathed thoughtfully, "a swig o' whiskey might not go bad."

"Lay still," Shade told him. "I'll be right back." He found his boots in the rubble near the pack rig and stamped into them. For the moment he pushed the bushwhacker out of his mind. Someone shouted as he raced around the corral, heading for the darkened Texas Bar.

"Stop there, or I'll shoot!"

Shade glimpsed the figure of Ludlow Finch standing near his own shack in his b.v.d.'s. The scrawny stableman continued to yell and gesture with what looked to be a long-barreled shotgun. Shade ignored him.

He considered the cottonwood door of the Texas Bar for only a moment, then, without preamble, kicked the flimsy barrier free of its chain and padlock.

Lamps were hurriedly lighted up and down the one-sided street. Someone, probably the bartender, began an outraged yelling from the back of the saloon. Shade ignored him as he had the stableman, fumbled behind the bar until he found a bottle that felt full, and turned again for the street.

Someone fired a pistol. It could have been any one of a dozen men who had already spilled into the street. But Shade was numb to gunfire, and everything else except a dying old man and a bottle of cheap whiskey.

A small white moon glowed high in the eastern sky, bathing the nervous citizenry with timid light. Shade pounded back around the corral, crossing once more in front of the still-yelling Finch.

"Potter!" Shade pulled up in front of the listing camp shack. "Potter, I can't vouch for how good a whiskey it is, but . . ."

Even before he stepped inside he knew that the old man was not listening. "Potter . . ." He knelt beside the old scout's bunk and struck a match. The mild old eyes gazed in blank wonder at the shattered front wall. Shade moved the match back and forth in front of the old man's face. The eyes continued to stare at that one fixed spot in mid-air. Gently, Shade closed Pleasant Potter's eyes. The match flickered out.

Until that moment Shade had given little thought to his brief relationship with the old scout. Now he thought about it. And he found it hard to believe that the passing of a near stranger could leave him feeling so cold-gutted and empty.

The male citizenry of Tribulation, in various states of undress, was gathered in the wagon yard, plaguing the night with a babble of excited questions. Who? How? Why?

The sound touched only the surface of Shade's senses. "I was a fool to of tied up to you in the first place," he said harshly to the still figure in the bottom bunk. "Hard-headed old buzzard. Why didn't you stay at Sill and live on your pension and forget about bein' a scout?" He answered the question with another one directed at himself. "And why don't *you* get railroadin' out of your system and take up a sensible trade?"

Maybe, he decided, the old man hadn't been so unlucky after all. At least he had cashed in on the job—which was probably more than would be said for Frank Shade.

The storekeeper, John Monday, put his head through the doorway and peered at Shade's lanky figure crouching near the old man. Monday cleared his throat nervously. "Ah . . . ever'body all right in there?"

Shade turned. "Fine and dandy," he said harshly.

The storekeeper blinked and stared wide eyed at the shambles. "What about Potter?"

Shade's knifelike grin was more searing than a curse. "There ain't nothin' wrong with Potter that an undertaker can't handle."

Monday, looking shocked, quickly withdrew his head. Shade, a voice—in a tone so changed that it sounded like a different language—said, "No more walkin' for you, old-timer. No more hurt from frostbit feet. No more bein' afraid that you'd outlived your time." He lifted the old man's body as if it were a child's, carried it outside the shack and laid it on a bed of loose straw near the corral.

Ludlow Finch, having gotten himself into pants and boots, started toward Shade. "I told you!" the stableman shouted angrily. "I warned you not to stay here tonight! But you wouldn't listen! You just had to go and be bullheaded about it, didn't you? Well, look at my camp shack there—who do you think's goin' to pay for *that?*"

Shade raked Finch with a steely glance, but the stable-man persisted. "I put it to you, Shade—who's goin' to pay for my camp shack? It's your fault, ain't it, that it got tore up? You admit that much, don't you?" The voice became wheedling. "After all, I *did* warn you, and you wouldn't listen. So who's goin' to pay? Right's right and fair's fair, and . . ."

Shade reached out and grasped a handful of Finch's b.v.d.'s and twisted the limp garment tight against the scrawny chest. "And dead's dead," he said softly.

Finch blinked. "Listen here, Shade, don't try to threaten me . . ."

"Shut up," Shade said in the same soft tone.

Ludlow Finch was not a perceptive man. He readily accepted a quiet voice as a sign of weakness. "You don't scare me, Shade. You pay for my camp shack or I aim to go after the deputy sheriff . . ."

Shade hit him. He hadn't meant to. The stableman was much older and smaller and weaker than Shade, but he hit him just the same. Reeling crazily, Finch staggered almost twenty yards before he fell. The good citizens of Tribulation stood like dark stones, looking first at Shade, then at the still figure of the stableman.

The moment of unleashed savagery had done him good. Shade could still feel the tingle in his fist. He turned hopefully to the others, but the stone figures did not move. The men of Tribulation decided it was not their problem. As if by some silent prearranged signal, they turned back toward town.

"Just a minute," Shade indicated the motionless stable-man. "Take him with you."

Two men, passively hostile, came forward grudgingly. They

lifted Finch between them and took him away without a word.

Shade discovered that he was so tense that the long muscles in his arms and shoulders were beginning to cramp. It had been a long time since he had felt like this, craving violence as some men craved whiskey, with every nerve in his big frame. He could tell himself that it was a stupid thing, hitting Finch, but he could not make himself regret doing it. It would turn the townsmen against him even more definitely than they had been before. For those rare ones who might have been teetering in the balance, this was just the thing to tip them over to the side of Brown. And still he did not regret it.

He looked down at Potter's dead face. "Sorry, old-timer. This is the best I can do for now." He shook out a gray and black striped Navajo saddle blanket and covered the old man.

III

Shade made no effort to locate the killer that night. First things first, he reminded himself. The old man had to be buried—then there would be time to think about the killer. "It ain't likely I'll forget you," he thought aloud, looking out at the night.

He made two more trips to the camp shack, bringing out the pack gear and the old man's plunder. Without a twinge of conscience he pulled down part of a doorframe and started a small fire a short distance from the old man's body. "Well," he said, "I guess this is where we sit out the night." He sat cross-legged in front of the fire, methodically built a smoke and lit it.

He recalled Potter's wry solution to the problem of locating Brown—simply offer themselves as targets so big and inviting that a bushwhacker wouldn't be able to resist taking a shot at them. Well, Shade thought bleakly, that's just what he was doing now. A drygulcher would never find a better target than the one he offered now, silhouetted against the hot light of a cottonwood fire.

But no more shots came out of the night. Shade uncorked the bottle that he had taken from the Texas Bar, silently saluted the old man and took a long, burning pull from the neck.

At regular intervals he would light a new smoke and take another pull at the bottle. Time and events of the night became blurred in his mind. Once Shade heard himself talking quietly, soberly to himself—as the old man had been in the habit of doing. "Empty gut," he said knowingly, nodding to the fire. "Maybe I better let the bottle rest a while."

But with the bottle set aside, his thoughts began to gather, focusing angrily on the murder of the old man. "That won't do," he thought. "Got to take it a step at a time." He gazed past the fire, at the dark shape of Tribulation. "Don't get me wrong, boys. It ain't that I'm throwin' in my cards. When I pull out of your fair little city, I'll have Brown with me—in a saddle or across one—or I won't pull out at all."

Shade turned his gaze upward, studying the subtle shift of moon and stars, and judged that it was near midnight. For almost four hours he had been sitting there thinking about a lot of things, but mostly about the killer. He had thought, before tonight, that he had known all about hating Brown. He hadn't known anything at all. A mere threat to his railroading ambitions had been a mild thing compared to what he felt now.

This realization came to Shade with something of a surprise. He hadn't thought that anything—no matter what—

could loom more important than his own ambition. It was
hard to understand. He and the old man had known each
other only a short time, they had not been particularly
close—and still . . . What had it been? Why did he get that
sickish, hollowed-out feeling in his gut every time he looked
at that blanket-covered figure and realized the old man was
dead?

Maybe it was something to do with guilt. Maybe, when
you got to the bottom of it, he was just being glad it was
the old man instead of himself that had taken the two bullets
in his chest.

No, it was more than that. Shade reached for the bottle
and solemnly studied the brownish liquid against the firelight. Slowly, the answer came to him. For the best part
of thirty-three years he had been gouging and clawing, fighting like a bitch wolf with new pups for every small advantage. When you're pulling yourself out of quicksand by
your own bootstraps, it doesn't leave a whole lot of time for
learning about people.

It was a sorry thing for a grown man to have to admit
to—but that old man had been about the nearest thing to
a friend that he had ever had.

Shade grinned sourly and started to uncork the bottle.
Suddenly he let the bottle drop and lunged away from the
fire. A dark figure of a man had moved out of the darker
shadows near the end camp shack. Scrambling toward the
outer edge of firelight, he had grabbed his Winchester and
had it ready to fire by the time he had rolled over the second
time. "Too damn slow!" he thought savagely. "If it was
Brown he would already have me dead!"

The figure halted beyond the ring of firelight. "*Ah-hi'ts*
. . ." The word was spoken quietly, almost hissed. The man
moved in a few steps to the exact edge of the light. "*Ah-
hi'ts*," he said again.

THE GRABHORN BOUNTY

Shade did not recognize the Comanche word for "friend," but he recognized the speaker. "White Dog? Is that you?"

The Indian grunted. Shade breathed easier as the young Kiowa stepped into the light, the broad, Mongol face impassive. He wore the casual dress of most young males of the plains tribes—a blue pull-over shirt, breechclout, and leggings. The night was warm and he had not bothered with a blanket.

The Indian glanced at the covered body and spoke again in Comanche. "*Ta'pave?*" Whites, as well as other Indians, found the Kiowa language impossible to master. When a Kiowa spoke to an outsider, it was usually in the court language of the plains, Comanche. "*Ta'pave?*" he asked again.

"Yes." Shade got to his feet and brushed himself off. He understood almost no Comanche, but this one word was known to many. It meant "everybody's brother," and the plains tribes had adopted it as a title of exceptional honor. The President of the United States was "*Ta'pave.*" And so had Pleasant Potter been.

White Dog gazed at the body but did not go near it. Shade recovered the bottle, pulled the cork and held it out to the Indian. "This ain't exactly accordin' to law, I guess, but you and the old man was pretty good pals, I guess. A little drink to send him off don't seem out of place."

White Dog knew only slightly more English than Shade knew Comanche, but he understood the proffered whiskey well enough. "*Chart,*" he said solemnly. "*Bosa-pah.*" He took the bottle, tilted it and drank steadily until it was empty. He flung the bottle into the night and sat cross-legged in front of the fire.

Shade stared wide-eyed. Luckily, the bottle had been less than a quarter full, but even so . . .

The men faced each other across the fire. After a while Shade said, "You and the old man was pretty good pals."

THE GRABHORN BOUNTY

White Dog tilted his face and gazed blankly at the pale moon. He was a young man, his memory did not reach back to the days when Pleasant Potter and the hated cavalry had warred against his people. But legend had it that the old man had been a worthy enemy, and White Dog could well believe it. After the days of war had passed, the scout had become a stout ally of the plains tribes, speaking for them at treaty meetings, arguing for them, sometimes angrily, in his own tongue. A strange man. Not like the Quakers who came to them preaching of a strange god and pressing them into farm schools—these nations of warriors and hunters.

Regarding the covered body, White Dog recalled that other whites had lived among the tribes briefly, but only Potter had seen them as nations of individuals. When White Dog had fallen sick with the young man's affliction, love, Potter had presented him with a fine pinto stallion to add to the dowry string. "Hell," he had shrugged. "I was young myself once, I reckon. Anyhow, livin' on a gover'ment pension, this old Appaloosa's about the only animal I can afford to keep."

The best part of an hour passed in silence. At last Shade said, "I can see this here's goin' to be a long night. Set tight, White Dog, I'll see if I can scare up a little more cheer."

Shade lurched to his feet and realized that he was already drunker than he had been for a long time. But not drunk enough. With elaborate erectness he again walked to the darkened Texas Bar. The door was open. Tom Murdles, the saloonkeeper, sat in the darkness with an old converted Starr revolver grasped in both hands. He sounded nervous. "I don't want no trouble, Shade!"

"Me neither," Shade said blandly. "Not right now, leastwise. All I want is another bottle of whiskey."

"They ain't none"—Murdles swallowed—"for sale."

Shade considered this for a moment. Even bartenders in

83

Tribulation were afraid to sell him whiskey. That was faintly interesting, but Shade was more interested in the liquor stock on the back shelf. He stood to one side of the door so that pale moonlight filtered into the room.

"Listen to what I tell you," Murdles said, licking his lips. "I've got a gun here. Just go off and leave me alone."

"For one night," Shade told the barkeep, "I've had a belly-ful of bein' shot at. If you've sure enough got a gun, and if you aim to use it, I advise you to do a good job with the first shot—it's liable to be the only one you'll get."

He put the timid barkeep out of his mind, blundering behind the bar until he found a bottle that satisfied him by its heft. He slapped some silver on the bar. "If that ain't enough, let me know and we'll settle up later, in daylight."

White Dog was still sitting cross-legged in front of the fire, his eyes almost closed, quietly chanting a song for the dead.

> *"If I roam, I will not roam forever.*
> *I won't be living here always.*
> *Only the sun lives here forever.*
> *Only the Earth remains forever."*

Shade did not understand the Kiowa words, but the solemn sound of the chant caused him to stop and stand back a few paces until it was finished. Then he pulled the cork on the new bottle and handed it to White Dog. "Not the whole damn bottle now. It's got to last us the rest of the night."

The Kiowa took the bottle, but this time a little ceremony went ahead of the drinking. He offered the bottle to the four sacred directions, and to the sky, and then he dribbled a little of the whiskey to the ground as an offering to the earth. Then he drank—three long swallows before Shade grabbed the bottle. Shade saluted the covered body, drank, and replaced the cork. "Guess we ought to be thinkin' about gettin' the old man planted," he said. "Can't leave him here for folks in Tribulation to bury. *That's* for sure."

White Dog sat for a long while in perfect silence. Then, without warning, he threw back his head and began to laugh. It was a wild cackling, almost a feminine sound, and Shade was properly startled. "I don't know how it is with you Kiowas, but wakes never struck me as bein' especially funny."

The young Indian cackled again, then leaped to his feet and began a highly animated dance around the circle of firelight. "You're drunk," Shade said with little sign of surprise. He lay back on his saddle and became interested in the intricate, mincing steps of the dance. "Well, old man," he thought aloud, "maybe this here's the kind of send-off you'd like."

He took another pull at the bottle and began to grin. He didn't know what he was grinning about. What he really wanted was to feel his hands about that bushwhacker's throat and strangle him very slowly. In the absense of someone to strangle, he grinned. And in the absence of a drum, he began beating his hands together, sliding sideways into the spirit of the dance.

The dance must have lasted a long while. From time to time White Dog would pause long enough to pull on the bottle. When the fire died down, Shade threw on more wood. There was a good deal of laughing and yelling. It occurred to Shade, later, that they had caused a pretty good commotion, for just the two of them. But nobody tried to stop them. Nobody ventured near the wagon yard.

Two hours before first light White Dog suddenly stopped dancing. He spoke briefly in Kiowa, then signed that he was going back to camp but would soon return.

Left alone with the body, Shade felt the bitterness returning. But the whiskey had numbed his brain. For the moment he could only stare blankly into the dying fire, unable to decide what his next move would be.

Perhaps half an hour had passed when he heard White Dog returning. This time the young Kiowa was not alone. Another, older Kiowa was with him. Also an old Comanche, a frail old man all bone and gristle and skin so old and leathery that it was almost black. They had with them a sturdy little paint stallion dragging a travois rig.

Shade peered at them blearily. "What's goin' on here?"

White Dog using his few words of English and much arm-swinging sign, explained that the Indians were taking the body to the reservation for burial. Shade groaned and rubbed his eyes. The period of soaring drunkenness was nearing an end—the violent afteraffects were just beginning.

He peered through his fingers at White Dog. "I don't know if I like this or not."

The young Kiowa went conveniently stupid and pretended not to understand. The other Kiowa and old Comanche gently lifted the body and placed it on the travois. Shade, after a moment, decided that it was probably the best thing. One thing was sure—he couldn't depend on the folks of Tribulation to give the old man much of a send-off. "Hold on a minute," he told the Indians. "I might as well get my gear and go with you."

He had already saddled the claybank and was setting the pack on the dun when he recalled the old man's last words. He brought the animals toward the fire which had now died down to a bed of coals. "This here's yours," he said, handing the old man's Henry over to the young Kiowa.

White Dog frowned and began gesturing and talking in Kiowa. The old Comanche, whose dark face had the collapsed look of the freshly scalped, came forward a little and spoke haltingly. "White Dog say why give rifle?"

Shade's head was beginning to pound. He gathered his

86

thoughts with difficulty. "The old man, Potter, says give the stuff over to White Dog. That's about the last he had to say before cashin' in." He squinted. "Where'd you learn to talk American?"

The old Indian ignored him and relayed the message to White Dog in the language of the Quahada Comanche. The young Kiowa looked at Shade, then stared straight ahead into the distance.

"There's the horse, too," Shade said. "The Appaloosa over in the horse pen. A fair to middlin' saddle, a good Navajo blanket, a pistol, and what little plunder you find in his warbag and pockets. The whole shootin' match belongs to White Dog now."

And a good piece of the Grabhorn bounty, he was about to say, when and if he managed to nail up Brown's hide. But that possibility seemed too far off and too full of ifs to talk about.

CHAPTER SIX

I

THE MIXED CAMP of Kiowas and Quahada Comanches and a scattering of Plains Cheyenne was situated on a sweet-water fork at the foot of the Wichitas. They had traveled the best part of a day since leaving Tribulation, and Shade was flannel-mouthed and sour with fatigue. A Cheyenne with a streak of vermilion down the part of his black hair met them a little way outside the village and directed them to his lodge.

The old Comanche, whose name was Eve-mora-yak'e, or Bull Frog, shouted at the gathering crowd and waved them all away except for a few who had been close personal friends of Potter. Then the members of the burial party got down, hunkered around an open fire in front of the Cheyenne's lodge. They motioned for Shade to join them as they speared chunks of meat from a brass kettle, eating silently after making an offering to the sacred directions.

Shade managed a sick grin and shook his head. His stomach was squeamish, and he suspected the meat in the kettle was boiled puppy, a great favorite of the Cheyennes.

From a distance a group of men watched in silence. The women began to wail. The burial detail finished the meal quickly, took the body from the travois and carried it inside the tepee to prepare for burial. Shade entered the tent with the others but there was little he could do but watch.

The Cheyenne, who was called Comes Running, began stripping off the old man's clothing—the ancient hunting shirt, the cavalry trousers, the blackened moccasins, all fell in a heap on the ground. White Dog bathed the body thoroughly. The face was carefully shaven and overlayed with vermilion, and the eyes were sealed with red clay.

They dressed the body in beautiful buckskin leggings and long shirt. On the dead toeless feet went soft moccasins, tasseled and beaded in green, the favorite color of the Cheyennes. Then, very gently, the men bent the stiffened legs, forcing the knees up beneath the chin. White Dog, his face like stone, quickly bound the corpse in this position with long, strong thongs of rawhide.

The Plains Indians did not delay burial after life had fled

a body. The old man was almost ready for his last ride—there were only a few last touches to be attended to. White Dog solemnly hung a beaded medicine bag around the old man's neck—a small buckskin pouch containing several sacred items to comfort an old man in a dark land. The old Comanche fixed a rare eagle feather to the sparse hair. Comes Running fixed about the dead waist a belt and sheath beaded in Cheyenne green, and a knife with a haft of green-veined stone.

The body was almost ready for burial.

White Dog threw back the lodge flap and made sign to the waiting crowd. This was the moment for relatives and close friends to view the body for the last time. The old man had no relatives but, it seemed, many friends. The young Kiowa posted himself in front of the lodge and directed the procession through the lodge. The women continued to wail.

At last Bull Frog and White Dog and Comes Running and Shade were alone once more with the body in the death lodge. They draped a new trade blanket over the body and bound it in place with rawhide thongs. At last they lifted the body between them, took it from the lodge and placed it in a sitting position on the Appaloosa which had been brushed and rubbed with grass until it shone. Two women—the mother of White Dog and another—rode on either side of the Appaloosa, holding the body in position.

The saddled claybank and three Indian ponies were brought to the lodge. Shade mounted with the others and became a part of the procession, climbing slowly into the abruptly rising peaks of the Wichitas.

Burial was done in the Comanche way, in a natural cave on the highest accessible peak. Gently, the body was lowered into a natural crevice, and the place covered with heavy stones. Finally a bleached buffalo skull was placed atop the stones to mark the place of burial.

The procession began the long trek down the rugged slopes, returning to the village. It was over. There was wailing among the women, but no violent period of mourning was to be expected. The death of a young warrior might well keep the entire village in a turmoil for weeks or months, but the passing of an old man—even one held in much affection—was a natural thing and could not be regarded as tragic. The Plains Tribes understood these things.

Shade did not. The old man had been murdered. That was the thing he could not forget. The knowledge lay like a darkening cloud bank along the horizon of his thoughts.

II

Deputy Sheriff Joe Hicks rode into Tribulation a little past noon. What was this he'd heard about a shooting?

The townsmen were quick to tell him—a blend of what they thought was safe and what they thought he wanted to hear. They showed the peace officer the demolished camp shack, which was now a litter of rawhide lumber on the ground. Ludlow Finch, in a rage, had given the shack a final kick which had brought it down.

Hicks regarded the site with dim interest. "Hell, boys," he said wearily, "there ain't nothin' I can do. You tell me there was a man shot here, killed, but there ain't no body. Any of you boys see a body? Well, without a body there just ain't been a killin'—speakin' legal, of course." He took a bite of fruited tobacco and chewed thoughtfully. "You fellers think on this a minute. Are you right sure this gent you seen was dead? Actual dead and not just playin' possum?"

The citizens of Tribulation shuffled uneasily. The night

before, John Monday, outraged at Shade's behavior, not to mention the reckless manner in which the unknown assassin had shot to pieces the camp shack, had sent his son to the county seat in search of a deputy. Now the storekeeper was not at all certain that he had done the right thing. Lawmen were notorious for the questions they asked. In Tribulation too many questions could get a man hurt, or even killed. To prove the point he had only to recall Horse-blanket Mary or Pleasant Potter.

But Potter had disappeared during the night.

Some of the townsmen noticed that most of the Indian camp had also disappeared. Potter had been notorious as a champion of Indians. It was simple enough to put the pieces together and guess what had happened.

"How about it, boys?" the deputy asked patiently. "Any of you got a notion where this 'dead man' could of wandered off to?"

The men said nothing.

"What about the one called Shade? Whereabouts did *he* get off to?"

The men gazed at one another, at the ground, the sky, everywhere but at the deputy. Joe Hicks, a middle-aged failure of a farmer who had accepted a deputy's star only to keep his family from starving, made no attempt to hide his relief. No sense borrowing trouble, poking into a killing when it couldn't even be proved that a killing had taken place. He would rest his horse overnight and ride back to the county seat in the morning. Obviously the men of Tribulation were sorry about calling him in the first place. It wasn't likely they would holler if he just left them to settle their troubles their own way.

The townsmen drifted away one and two at a time. Finch, the stableman, was the last to go.

"What about my camp shack?" he demanded. "Who's goin' to pay for *that?*"

Hicks grinned. "The gent that nobody saw that killed the dead man that got up and wandered off durin' the night I reckon."

The stableman's face glowed angrily. "Listen here, it's your duty to . . ." He stopped suddenly, breaking off in mid-sentence. Hicks watched curiously as Finch darted nervous glances up and down the line of shacks—almost as if he were afraid of someone overhearing his words. "Forget it," he growled to no one in particular. "That shack wasn't worth nothin' anyhow."

The stableman stamped off toward the corral. The deputy sighed. A curious town. And a nervous one. He would be just as glad to see the last of it.

He prowled aimlessly through the rubble. What had happened was perfectly clear. Even an untrained mind could figure it out. The camp shack riddled as if by a Gatling gun. From the looks of things, the shooting had come from the weed patch to the west of the wagon yard, somewhere behind the Drover's Cafe.

Hicks nudged a brown spot in the dirt with the toe of his boot. Blood. Two empty whiskey bottles near a mound of cold ashes—the site of a wake. Why else would a person sit for hours in the night air drinking up two bottles of green whiskey?

So there had been a shooting, a killing. And the man named Shade had held a wake, but not alone, drinking two bottles of Texas Bar whiskey at one sitting. No, Shade had been accompanied by person or persons unknown—Hicks smiled to himself at the professional ring of the phrase. Also, there were the travois tracks. The twin ruts in the ground that trailed off to the south. And the unshod prints of Indian pony. A few more parts of the mystery fell into place.

THE GRABHORN BOUNTY

So the Indians had come in the night and taken the body away. Nothing so much wrong in that, though. Indians liked to give their kind a good send-off—and old Potter had been a squaw man. So Shade and some Indians had sat around getting lit up on rotgut whiskey and decided to haul the old man off and give him a decent planting, which they were pretty sure he wouldn't get in Tribulation.

The deputy chewed steadily, his heavy jaws working to the slow rhythm of his thinking. What he wanted to do was get rested up for the ride back to the county seat where he would make his report to the sheriff. The old man was dead. That was that. Nothing could be done about it. The killer, probably a professional, was already out of the county, more than likely. Potter had tramped on tender toes, somewhere down the line. He had got himself killed for his trouble.

So let it alone, Hicks told himself. Killings like this happened all the time, and they never got solved. Why wear himself out over nothing?

Still, it was a dull day and there was nothing else to do . . . With a curiosity so faint that it bordered on indifference, he strode toward the patch of green mullein. After several minutes of tramping back and forth in the weeds he came to an abrupt stop and grunted.

Here the weeds were flattened and wilted. This is where the bushwhacker had hid out to do his killing. A flashing star of light caught the deputy's eye, and he quickly scooped up the metal cartridge case. "Well, now," he said aloud, "Mr. Killer's got hisself a Henry. And not a very new one, either. A .44 caliber, rimfire. Hell, the Yankees was usin' them in the war. . . ."

He pocketed the cartridge case and searched the area for more. He found fifteen of them, as they had been ejected from the rifle. The killer had come with his magazine full and ready for business, all right. But taken all in all, it was pretty shoddy work for a professional. Fifteen rounds of ammunition spent and only one body to show for it all. Shoddy.

Joe Hicks pocketed his find, went to the Drover's Cafe and ate a heavy meal of boiled beans and a dry salt meat, then tramped up the street to the Texas Bar and took a glass of whiskey to settle the food.

The cafe owner and bartender regarded him narrowly, as though he might have the plague. Wherever he went, customers automatically disappeared. They weren't giving him much chance to ask questions.

Well, the town looked quiet enough now. A little too quiet, for the deputy's taste—it was beginning to remind him of the silence of a graveyard.

But it was none of his business. The citizens of Tribulation had taken it out of his hands. A little before sundown he returned to the wagon yard, rented one of Finch's camp shacks and went to sleep with a clear conscience.

III

Deputy Sheriff Hicks awoke before first light with the scalp-prickling feeling that he was not alone in the shack. He started to reach for his rifle when something small, cold, and round touched his throat.

"Don't grab, mister." The voice sounded grimly amused. "It ain't polite."

The muzzle of a pistol bored into Hicks' throat. It was as dark as tar inside the shack. The man was only an indistinct darkness against a blacker darkness. He spoke again, "You the county sheriff that come down here to look into the accident?"

"I ain't the sheriff," Hicks croaked. "Just the deputy." He tried to swallow, but the muzzle bored harder into the hollow of his throat. "What . . . what accident you talkin' about?"

"The accident that happened to the old scout."

Hicks could sense a grin behind the voice. Accident! Fifteen rifle shots fired deliberately into a flimsy cabin. The deputy tried but could not speak, because of the pressure of the muzzle. The invisible man hadn't meant him to speak —he already knew all he needed to know. "I want to give you some friendly advice, deputy," the voice went on mildly. "Throw your rig together and get out of Tribulation before sunup. It'll save me some trouble—and you some dyin'."

The man made a small sound, almost a sigh. "Just to show you I'm talkin' business . . ." The pressure was removed from the deputy's throat. Hicks imagined that he could hear the swish of the gunbarrel as it split the still air of the shack—but that could have been a trick of the mind that happened later. All that he remembered for sure was a ꟼash of pain, and then a deeper darkness.

IV

It was a little past daybreak when Shade returned to Tribulation, sour with fatigue, red-eyed from want of sleep. The old man had had a first-class Indian burial—it was all over now. But it was not over in Shade's mind.

He reined in at the wagon yard, almost hoping that Finch would take a try at stopping him. But the stableman did not make an appearance. The town, in the steely light of a prairie dawn, seemed to be holding its breath.

Shade got down and began to unsaddle when he noticed that one of the cabins was occupied. Curiously, he walked down the line a few paces and peered through the open doorway. Maybe, he thought, Horseblanket Mary had taken a turn for the better and come home.

It was not Mary. The occupant of the shack was a thickset man in his middle forties. Completely dressed except for boots, he sat on the side of his bunk holding his bloody head in his hands.

Shade stepped cautiously across the threshold. "You must be a stranger in these parts. Tribulation is a hard place on strangers."

The deputy peered uncertainly at Shade's homely face. There was a sizable bruise on his forehead, and a three-inch cut that had done a good deal of bleeding before it had dried over. There was dried blood on the bunk and even a little on the wall.

Shade regarded the deputy's star on the stranger's hardworn vest. He felt for makings, hunkered down against the doorframe and leisurely built a smoke. "Seems like lawman's a scarce breed in Greer County—guess I never expected to see one here in Tribulation."

"Mister," Hicks said shakily, "I ain't no lawman. I'm just a stove-up farmer that took the badge so's to put some beans in my kids' bellies." After a moment he added, "You must be the one called Shade."

Shade nodded, lighting his smoke.

"I don't know what your trouble is," the deputy said. "And I don't much care, if you want the truth of it. I've had a gutful of Tribulation. They called me down on a killin', but when I got here there wasn't any body. The law can't investigate killins without there's a body somewheres."

Shade looked at him steadily, tried to figure him out. After the shooting somebody in a panic had called for the law. A mistake that, by this time, someone would be regretting. "There was a killin'," Shade said tonelessly. "My partner. An old buzzard named Potter. The Indians and me, we took him up in the Wichitas and buried him."

Hicks shook his head, wincing. "I still ain't seen a body," he said doggedly. "There ain't a thing I can do."

"Sure there is," Shade said flatly. "You can crawl out of town with your tail between your legs. If I locate the gent that buffaloed you, maybe I'll let you know." He got to his feet, snapped his cigarette through the open doorway, then left the shack.

It was near noon when Shade came awake, fully clothed and sweat soaked, on one of Finch's bunks. His Winchester was on the bunk beside him. His revolver was in his hand, ready at full cock. "When you get yourself ready for company," he thought, "looks like it never comes."

He sat up slowly, still tired but not as tired as he had been earlier. He wondered if the rifleman and the deputy's buffaloer were one and the same. Probably. Everything that had happened, even this attack on Hicks, was connected with his search for Brown.

Brown . . . So much had happened, so much gall had been spilled, he had almost forgotten that at the bottom of the old man's murder was that same familiar name. Brown.

He was surprised to find the deputy outside the shack, sitting on the ground with his back against the plank wall, holding a Winchester saddle gun across his lap.

"Figured you'd be headed back to headquarters before now," Shade said dryly, "seein' there's no law business to hold you in Tribulation."

The deputy grinned faintly and looked as though it hurt

his wounded head. "You looked some tuckered. Thought I'd kind of keep a watch on things while you rested up."

"Mighty decent," Shade drawled. He was puzzled. There wasn't much doubt that somebody in Tribulation would like to kill him—and it was just possible that the deputy's standing watch had saved him from getting the same as Pleasant Potter had got. He went to the corral and washed at the pump. When he came back the deputy was still there.

Shade put all his questions in one word. "Why?"

Hicks shrugged. He had an ointment-soaked rag bound around his head, causing his hat to teeter delicately at every movement. "Don't reckon you'd believe me if I told you I just wanted to do my duty and try to see that nobody else gets killed."

"I wouldn't believe you," Shade told him.

The deputy climbed slowly and carefully to his feet. "Maybe if I told you I'd heard about the Grabhorn bounty . . ."

Shade's eyes glittered. "Now I believe you. One thing folks around here understand is money." His gaze narrowed. "How much do you know?"

"Just that the Grabhorns have a bounty posted, a big one, on the thieves that have been robbin' their express cars. I nosed around town some, talked to an old woman down at the Indian camp and to some Tribulation menfolks, and to a pair of cowhands from Pot Allard's Roman Three. Nobody was very talkative, except the cowhands. They knowed all about you and what you was doin' in these parts. You been askin' about a man name of Brown."

"Brown's just somethin' I call him by," Shade said suspiciously. "I guess you know that he killed an express agent not long ago. And more'n likely he's the one that killed my partner."

Hicks nodded, holding his hat on his head with both

hands. "I'll tell you how it is with me, Shade. I've got a wife and four kids and a lamed-up mule, and most of the time all of them are hungry. I ain't brave, and I ain't much of a manhunter, but I need the money. If you figure this express robber, this Brown, is in these parts, I guess you've got good reason. I aim to start lookin' for him. We can work together, or on our own. That's up to you."

Shade studied the man and decided he meant exactly what he said. "I've been doggin' Brown's trail for the best part of two years. What makes you think you could earn a share of that bounty money?"

The deputy dug into his pocket and produced the handful of cartridge cases. "Here's somethin' for a start. I found them over in the mullein patch behind the cafe."

Shade took the glistening brass tubes, held them in both hands as if they were still hot. They were exactly like the cases he had found after the first bushwhacking. Two of them had held slugs that were now in the dead body of Pleasant Potter. But now they could tell him nothing. They were just spent ammunition, perfectly clean and bright, except for bits of red clay that still clung to them.

"You've already had a taste of the way Brown works," Shade said, indicating Hicks' bandaged head. "You sure you've got the stomach for another helpin', or worse, if it comes?"

"The only thing I'm sure about is the money. I want it."

There was a frankness there that Shade found agreeable. It might just be that Hicks wanted that money bad enough to be of some help. It wasn't the bounty that Shade was interested in now—it was Brown.

"There's somethin' else," the deputy said. "While you was asleep, there was a woman askin' for you. Name of Durell."

Shade was surprised, and showed it. "What did she want?"

Now Hicks was looking at Shade in a curious way. "She

99

didn't say and I didn't ask. Figured you'd know. Anyhow, one of Pot Allard's hands brought her to town after supplies, in a buckboard." His thoughts turned inward for a moment. "Right pert little thing, no bigger'n a minute . . ."

"Don't forget the wife and kids," Shade said dryly. "Anyhow, she belongs to Pot Allard, and Allard don't take much to competition."

The deputy's heavy jowls warmed with color. "What I started to say, this woman, Miss Durell, caught me over by the corral and asked if I knowed you. She wants to talk to you. Private. She's takin' the buckboard back home by herself. She aims to stop at a creek about two miles west of here, in the reservation. There's a big grove of cottonwoods— that's where she wants to see you."

Shade didn't understand it. Why didn't she come to him directly? Why did she have to go through Hicks and then arrange a secret meeting over in the reservation? He squinted at the deputy.

"She must have heard somewheres that we was both here at the wagon yard," Hicks said. He closed his eyes, apparently intent on the throbbing in his head. "She did mention somethin' about you comin' out to their place the other day to see Allard."

A tenseness grabbed the muscles in Shade's shoulders, pulling him erect. Everything was beginning to point to Allard. First the rifle. Then the Roman Three hands that were in town unusually late on the night that Horseblanket Mary was beaten. Now it was Bess Durrell, wanting to talk to him about Allard.

Shade didn't know why. Maybe Bess was afraid of Allard. Maybe she hated him for driving off all the younger suitors. Or maybe Bess Durell had also heard about the Grabhorn bounty and wanted to make a deal.

Shade hoisted his riding gear and started for the corral.

"Just a minute," Hicks called. "Are we workin' together or ain't we?"

Shade hesitated only an instant. He needed all the help he could get. All he had to lose was part of the bounty money—and money was not important if you had to trade your life to get it. "We work together."

CHAPTER SEVEN

I

THE CREEK was almost dry, sapped lifeless by a heavy growth of salt cedar along the banks. The stand of cottonwoods mentioned by Hicks completely filled a wavering U bend in the meandering stream.

Shade, in spite of himself, felt his breathing come a little faster as he neared the green of the timber. He had seen Bess Durell only once, and then briefly, but there were women who could leave their stamp on a man with a single glimpse. Apparently this daughter of a down-and-out nester was such a woman.

Shade forded the shallow stream less than a thousand yards inside the reservation. This was something that Shade had wondered about—the Durell place was a good mile to the south and back on the other side of the line. That would make two miles that Bess had driven out of her way. Was the cover of timber that important? Was she that afraid that someone would see her talking to a railroad man?

He halted the claybank near the edge of the rattling cottonwoods. "Miss Durell . . ." He waited for perhaps half a minutes. He listened to a soft breeze moving through the pale green foliage. A background whirring of July flies rose from a nearby stand of weeds. Some small furry thing scampered up a tree and vanished like smoke. All the commonly unheard sounds of the prairie—and Shade was acutely aware of them. But there was not the sound of Bess Durell answering his call.

He nudged the claybank and rode toward the heart of the timber. Sunlight sparkled on glossy leaves; the ground was a shifting dapple of light and shadow, playing tricks with his eyes. He called again.

"Miss Durell, it's me, Frank Shade . . ."

Still no answering call. Shade could feel the sweat on the back of his neck turning cold. In railroad camps, where the best part of the population stood ready and willing to slip a knife between your ribs, a man soon developed a nose for danger.

Shade could smell it now, steely, dry, combustible. Cautiously, he kneed the claybank between the trees, wondering a little about that wide-eyed innocence of Bess Durell. He was liking this green grove less all the time, for reasons that he couldn't detail at the moment.

From what little he had seen of her, it was hard to think of Bess Durell setting anybody up for ambush. Hicks might do it, if there was enough money in it. Maybe that yarn about talking to the girl was just that, a yarn. Rattle enough silver in front of a man like Hicks and he'd likely do anything you asked. And Brown had never been close with money.

Shade brought the claybank to another halt. "What I ought

to do," he thought grimly, "is get out of here. Turn and run like a thief!"

He didn't do it. In the first place, the trees were so thick that hurrying was out of the question. Too, the thought of looking the fool in front of Bess Durell somehow rankled him. He didn't know why. Never before had he minded the way things appeared.

Going against his training and experience, he had talked himself out of beating an undignified retreat.

He decided to call once more. If Bess Durell was where she was supposed to be, she would hear him.

"Miss Durell!"

There was still no answer. And Shade knew there would not be one. For just a moment the prairie seemed to sigh. The July flies interrupted their whirring for just an instant —or was that Shade's imagination? No matter. The prickling sensation across his scalp would not be denied.

In what seemed one continuous motion, he grabbed his carbine, kicked free of the stirrups, raked the claybank cruelly with his spur rewels, and pitched out of the saddle. Before he fell he glimpsed a movement in the weeds near the creek. The startled animal went blundering through the trees. A pencil of flame spurted from the dark green mullein.

Shade could almost feel the hot breath of the slug as it slammed into a tree and richocheted crazily through the timber. "Close," Shade thought bleakly with some small, disengaged fraction of his brain. "They come a little closer every time."

With his conscious mind he was aware of falling, and at the same time watching anxiously for breath of white smoke that would mark the bushwhacker's position. He saw it just before he struck the ground with bone-rattling force. He couldn't afford the luxury of pausing to get his breath. He scrambled for the dubious cover of a young cottonwood, holding tightly to his Winchester.

The rifle sounded again, strangely muffled in the heavy foliage. The bullet whipped through the weeds several feet over Shade's head and to his right. It was not a show of bad marksmanship on the assassin's part. In this jungle of timber and weeds, it was not possible to line up a shot of more than a distance of twenty feet.

Shade, in order to fire on the other's position, would have to stand up and expose himself. And he was in no mood for suicide.

Neither, apparently, was the bushwhacker. The green grove relaxed its tense silence that had followed the two rifle shots. The whirring of July flies began again with great vigor. A light breeze rattled the big cottonwoods. Everything was as it had been before. The prairie ignored the two men lying so grimly intent in the weeds.

Silent seconds became minutes. Shade's muscles began to cramp. He started violently at every small sound. His finger had tightened involuntarily on the trigger, until the Winchester's hammer was almost ready to fall.

If he had any advantage at all, it was that the bushwhacker didn't know his exact position. What had started as a routine killing had developed into a waiting game. The first one to tire of waiting, disclosing his position, would be the loser.

Shade made himself relax. A hot sun, still hours high, blinked through the cottonwoods. Maybe, Shade told himself, if he could hold the standoff until dark, he could break off from the assassin and make his way back to Tribulation. There were certain questions that he would like very much to put to Deputy Hicks.

Shade was mildly surprised to realize that he did not want to break it off. It had occurred to him earlier, and now he felt it stronger than ever—his luck was about due to run out. Three drygulching attempts, and three times he had walked away. A man couldn't rightly ask for much more than that.

Anyhow, something told Shade that the other rifleman would not be eager to break it off. Three tries, and three misses. His pride must be pretty ruffled by this time.

Lying on his belly, the Winchester at the ready, Shade tried to judge the distance that lay between them. About thirty yards, he guessed. Maybe a little less. After all the time and trouble of trailing Brown, had the gap actually narrowed down to a bare thirty yards?

Shade breathed deeply. "Chew it slowly," he told himself. "Don't let it choke you."

So close, so close. And there was so little he could do. Lay still, he repeated to himself. And wait for Mr. Brown to make the first move.

Time dragged. Shade's arms began to cramp again. He glanced up at a blinking sun that seemed to be standing still. Doubts began to gnaw at him.

Was the assassin really Brown? The longer he thought about it the harder it was to believe. How could a girl like Bess Durell have anything to do with Brown? On the other hand, what kind of girl *was* Bess Durell? Was she innocent of the whole thing? Had Hicks used her name merely as bait to lure Shade into a trap? There were too many questions and not enough answers.

Over to Shade's right the sound of a snapping twig sounded like breaking bones. He shifted quickly, bringing the Winchester to bear on the sound. But there was only more weeds, more trees. No Brown. But Shade was certain that he had heard movement in the weeds. Had Brown got enough of waiting?

There was a faint thud, the sound of something striking

the ground off to Shade's left. Brown was chunking small pieces of bark or wood to draw Shade's attention away from his position. Shade felt along the ground, found a small twig and lobbed it over to one side. Two could play at this game.

The sound of movement was more pronounced now. Shade had to make himself lie still until Brown had declared himself. He squinted at the green wall of weeds until his eyes began to jump. There was still no sign of Brown. Then, by bare chance, Shade lifted his gaze and was suddenly staring straight into the muzzle of the assassin's rifle.

Shade froze. He realized that he had not the slightest chance of beating the assassin to the shot. He tried, but knew all the time that it was no use. The bushwhacker, shucking his boots, had climbed a cottonwood to its first low fork, and from that vantage point had Shade in his sights at point-blank range. Surprisingly, Shade found himself studying the man in detail, even as he struggled to bring the Winchester to firing position.

The smooth, bland face shocked him almost as much as the businesslike rifle in the man's slender hands. The pale eyes watching him impassively over the sights. The delicate mouth smiling faintly. "Brown?"

Shade heard himself speaking the name in a puzzled tone, and then in fury. "Brown!"

The slender trigger finger started its squeeze. Shade was still a full second away from firing—the assassin had all the time in the world. He was going to make up for those three misses. This time he would make absolutely sure that his man was dead.

Then another rifle sounded from the direction of the creek. Not Shade's, not the assassin's—one that neither had been aware of until that moment. Shade grunted, startled, as the bullet ripped from the heavy brush along the creekbank. But the bushwhacker was more startled. The bullet struck him squarely in the chest. Stunned, Shade saw the small black hole appear between the buttons on the man's shirt. Almost instantly the hole was ringed in scarlet.

The man dropped his rifle and started to fall backward. He grabbed the thick limbs of the fork for a moment, glaring hatred at Shade. Perhaps he never fully understood that Shade had not somehow, impossible as it had seemed, shot him before he could finish his trigger squeeze. A bloody froth bubbled at the corners of that finely drawn mouth. His hold loosened. And this time he fell, a dead weight plunging backwards out of the fork.

Shade, still numb from the suddenness of the action, rose to his knees in time to see White Dog breaking from the brush. The young Kiowa came toward Shade, not bothering to glance toward the tree where the assassin had fallen. White Dog carried Pleasant Potter's old Henry in both arms, as if it were a child. A whisper of white smoke still drifted up from the muzzle.

Shade's mouth was powder dry. "White Dog," he managed, "I don't know what brought you here, but . . ." The Kiowa paused only for a moment, looked at him flatly, then marched on to the forked tree. He stood for several long, harsh seconds staring down at the body of Handsome Corry.

CHAPTER EIGHT

I

WHITE DOG—with the distorted features of a sun dancer—stared for what seemed a long time at the body of Pot Allard's gunhand. Shade, still with that hollow gutted feeling, pushed through the weeds to the Indian's side.

Suddenly the Kiowa spat and Shade glimpsed the shimmering hate behind those dark eyes. He groped for English words but could find only one.

"Kill *Ta'pave!*" He spat again at the body.

Ta'pave—"Everybody's Brother." The name the Plains tribes had given to Pleasant Potter. Shade breathed deeply, thoughtfully. "That's the way it looks, White Dog. Killin' from ambush, that's about Handsome Corry's size, all right. But the old man—*Ta'pave*—was a tough old buzzard. That old Henry that he left you—it's almost like the old man crawled out of the grave hisself to settle the score."

White Dog understood, but understanding did little to dilute the stone-faced grief. A few years ago he would have scalped Corry as a matter of course, and then he or his squaws would have mutilated the body so that Corry's spirit could not plague him in the afterlife. But the days of scalping and mutilating were over—such things could mean bad medicine for the whole tribe. He had to content himself with spitting and hating.

"White Dog . . ." Shade studied the young Indian. "I'm mighty glad you turned up when you did—but how come you to do it? Because of the old man—*Ta'pave?*"

White Dog nodded.

"How'd you know where to find me? Did you trail me out of Tribulation?"

Once more the Indian nodded.

Shade sighed. A Kiowa killing a white man, especially on Comanche land that had been leased to Allard, could also be bad medicine.

Apparently White Dog had read his thoughts. His right hand shot out, palm down, waist high. The hand doubled, then the fingers flipped out violently several times. Shade recognized the sign for "bad," or "evil," as White Dog indicated the dead gunhand.

Well, Shade told himself, White Dog had had his reasons, and now it was done. Shade grinned wearily. "I thank you for what you done, White Dog. And the old man would too, if he could talk. But you better high-tail now—go to your own folks for a spell. I'll attend to Corry."

White Dog was aware of the trouble he could bring down on his tribe. With a stiff nod he started to leave, then he hesitated. Quickly he touched fingers to his eyes, then pointed toward the creek, or the prairie beyond the creek. He spoke harshly in his own tongue, gesturing widely.

Shade understood no Kiowa at all and very little sign, but he gathered that White Dog had seen something from his position on the creekbank. Something that had happened before the shooting. Out of all the arm-swinging gestures, Shade understood only one, the unmistakable sign for "woman." Not the Quaker agent's approved behind-the-head sign, indicating flowing hair. White Dog used the old sign that Indians used among themselves, one that left no room for doubt.

Shade frowned. "You saw a woman? When? Where?"

The Kiowa shrugged. He had spoken. If Shade could not understand sign talk, it was no fault of his. He turned away, and this time he walked straight for the heaviest brush along the creekbank. Shade caught a glimpse of the old man's Appaloosa as White Dog reined north through the trees.

Shade was alone with the body of the man that had tried to kill him. The murderer of the old man, and no telling how many others. Was it possible that this man, Handsome Corry, had been Brown?

Shade wouldn't believe it. It left too many loose ends. Maybe Corry had been on Brown's payroll. . . . That would explain the bushwhackings.

Then the rifle on the ground, Corry's rifle, caught Shade's attention. First he nudged it with his foot. Then, with a grunt, swooped down and picked it up.

It was a Winchester .44-40, not a Henry as Shade had expected.

Could it be possible that all the shootings were unrelated? Shade wouldn't believe that either. But how was he to explain this Winchester, when the other drygulch attempts had been with a Henry?

Then, along the edges of his senses, Shade heard someone coming toward him through the trees.

"Handsome! Where are you?"

Shade froze. He had never heard the voice before—and yet there was no doubt in his mind as to who the newcomer was.

"Handsome . . ." A light, soft, pleasing voice. A voice like music, Shade might have said, if he had had a romantic turn of mind. So this was the woman that White Dog had referred to. And her name was Bess Durell.

"Handsome, answer me!" She was slightly breathless from struggling against the barrier of weeds. Also she was a little vexed at having received no answer to her calls. Possibly she was just a little worried.

She appeared suddenly from behind an almost solid cluster of cottonwoods. Her mouth was half-open, words were at her lips, but they died instantly when she saw Shade. She made a startled sound, stepped back quickly and almost fell in a tangle of briars.

"What's the matter, Miss Durell? Wasn't you expectin' me?" Shade's words were edged to steel. He knew a kind of anger that was totally foreign to him. He had never wanted to strike a woman before.

She stared at him, wide-eyed, not yet noticing the body of Handsome Corry.

"You *did* tell that deputy sheriff, didn't you," Shade pressed, "that you wanted to talk to me?"

She appeared stunned. The pink tip of her tongue licked slowly around the deeper pink of her lips.

"Well," Shade said harshly, "here I am, Miss Durell. When you're ready to talk I'm ready to listen."

Still she said nothing. She couldn't seem to move her gaze from his face. She was much as Shade remembered her from that one brief glimpse—maybe just a bit smaller, just a bit more frail and childlike. Even now, with the facts so clear, he found that his core of anger was crumbling. He didn't want to hate her. He didn't want to believe that she had deliberately drawn him into these trees to be killed.

For a moment he would not speak for fear that she would sense his weakness. He merely stared at her with glazed eyes. Hers was a beauty that men would want to protect, not abuse. A beauty that had trapped half the men

111

in Tribulation, from what Handsome Corry had said that day. Now it had trapped Corry himself, in an unexpected way that seemed particularly just. The assassin had himself been assassinated.

Had she read his thought? Her stunned look changed to one of alarm. She stepped forward, cautiously, and stared directly at the body. She did not make a sound. Once she pressed her knuckles to her mouth and glanced at Shade, but she made no sound.

Shade's thoughts were traveling full circle. All he had to do was remember the old man, and his anger was as fresh and hot as before. "Well," he said flatly, "ain't you got anything to say, Miss Durell? You got to admit that I went to some trouble gettin' here. Just what is it that's so important . . ."

At last she spoke, and even her voice was the voice of a child. "How . . . How . . . I don't understand." She indicated the body, shuddered, and turned away.

"There ain't anything to understand," Shade heard himself saying. "Handsome there had a notion to kill me, but he got hisself killed instead."

She made a small, thin sound and pressed her knuckles to her eyes. Shade was unmoved. There was something fake about the gesture, as though she had been practicing it in front of a looking glass. In a very dim way he was beginning to understand Bess Durell. She began to sob. But Shade could see no tears.

"I'd admire to know," he said dryly, "just what it is about me that you don't like—so much that you want to see me dead."

"I don't know what you mean!" she cried. The voice was that of a tortured, bewildered child. Still, in Shade's ears, it sounded fake.

"You know," he told her. "You set up this little bushwhack when you gave that deputy a message to pass along to me."

"I didn't!"

"Sure you did," he went on monotonously. "You lined me up for Handsome's bullet. Now I'd like to know why."

Her sobs became louder. She ground her knuckles into her eyes until they were red.

Shade sighed. "You might as well tell me, Miss Durell. There's that deputy sheriff at Tribulation, and the Army up at Sill, not to mention the federal marshals around these parts—they're all goin' to take an interest in this."

Her sobbing stopped as suddenly as it had started. Wide-eyed, she stared at him. "You . . . you can't think that *I* had anything to do with this!"

"Right now I'm thinkin' a lot of things—but mostly I'm wonderin' how a girl like you could be mixed up in . . ."

A girl like her. What kind of a girl was that? Why didn't he simply bundle her up and take her to Tribulation to see the deputy. Then the bunch of them could take a trip to Sill and talk to the Army. The Provost had ways of dealing with intruders—he would soon get to the bottom of things.

It occurred to Shade that the notion wasn't as good as it would seem. Two men had been killed, one of them on Indian land, and Shade had been on hand both times. That was a fact that any provost worth his salt would find curious. Also, it was known at Sill that Shade had been tracking big bounty. Maybe he hadn't liked the notion of a stove-up old scout like Potter horning in for part of the scalp money—so Shade had killed him. As for Corry, the mercenary—maybe he had guessed or heard something that would be damaging to Shade, so Shade had killed him too, from ambush.

That was the way the Army mind would think, and Shade couldn't much blame them. He had to confess that it didn't seem possible that he had come out of the wagon yard shooting untouched. Also, this cottonwood grove was on leased range. Corry had a legal right to be here, being a hand of Allard's. But not Shade. A provost, even a friendly one, wouldn't have much trouble making a case out of that.

Of course, there was the girl to be considered, but on second thought her presence here didn't look so damaging. Corry, being a hand of Pot Allard's, had ridden with her from Tribulation as far as the reservation. After separating, Corry had headed for the cottonwoods to water his horse in the creek. A short time later Bess Durell had heard gunfire in the distance, and, on impulse, she had turned her buckboard toward the shooting.

Shade could hear it now—Bess Durell telling that story to a bunch of womanless Army men, looking frail and innocent as a new chick, batting those wide eyes at them in a brave attempt to hold back the tears. Yes sir, Shade could already hear it. Just the way he could hear the carpenters' hammers working on his gallows.

And Bess was beginning to hear it too. Shade saw her quickly recover from the shock of seeing Corry's body. "Just what," she asked—not arrogantly, but not timidly either— "am I supposed to be mixed up in, Mr. Shade?"

"I meant," he said wryly, "that it's too bad you had to get mixed up in a thing like this. It ain't a pretty sight."

She looked at him unblinkingly. Shade half-expected her to laugh, but she only said, "What do you intend to do now, Mr. Shade?"

What did she expect him to do, Shade wondered. Shoot her, maybe, and bury both bodies there on the creekbank? There was actually only one thing to do. Obviously she had not seen the shooting and knew nothing about White Dog.

Wearily, he said, "Go on back to your buckboard, Miss

Durell. I'll bring the . . . body along behind, soon's I catch the horses."

She looked at him in frank surprise. "The man you killed . . ." She indicated the body but would not look at it. "He was a top hand on the Roman Three payroll."

Was she warning him that Pot Allard would have him killed at the earliest possible moment, because the gunhand was dead? Shade couldn't be sure. The mind behind that childlike expression was a good deal more complex than it seemed.

II

The day was going poorly for Deputy Sheriff Joe Hicks. It was one thing to deal with rowdy cowhands, and now and then a tanked-up Indian—it was something else to mess with killers that liked to lie in ambush and cut you down from behind. Hicks had never pretended to be brave. Maybe life wasn't perfect, but he had a notion to hang onto it as long as he could.

A strong, loud voice from the depths of his bowels kept saying, "Get away from here. You're just a deputy sheriff, and you've got no obligation to stay where you're not wanted."

Another voice, this one in his head, was saying, "Think of that bounty. Think of all the things you could do with that money." In the end the voice in his head shouted down the one in his guts. It always came out that way—his need for money was more powerful than his fear of dying.

Maybe "honesty" wasn't the word to describe Joe Hicks. It was something more common than that—a weariness of grubbing his life away in this country of mesquite soil and gyp water, of never seeing enough meat in the pot . . .

At any rate he was honest enough to admit that his staying here had nothing at all to do with "duty," or any other high-flown notion—it all boiled down to a matter of cash money.

But the money wasn't his yet—a long way from it. He would have to work for it, and maybe do a little bleeding—on these points he didn't try to fool himself.

III

The Indian camp was almost deserted. White man's problems could only mean trouble to Indians. They had quietly slipped back to the reservation to wait for the thing to blow over, or for the principles to kill one another. This possibility caused much hopeful speculation and a great deal of amusement among the Comanches and Kiowas.

Only the gambling lodge and three or four others were left standing. The pony herd was gone. Great brown circles dotted the prairie, marking the places where tepees had stood. Joe Hicks, riding around the bare circles, as though the tepees were still there, heard the barking of a single dog, and then nothing. The place was as silent as a plague camp.

Horseblanket Mary was on her feet but in foul humor. She hobbled to the open flap of the gambling tent as Hicks reined up in front. "Git away from me!" she spat, hugging her injured ribs. "Can't you see what your meddlin's already done!" There was an alcoholic glitter in her small eyes. Obviously she had been using Shade's whiskey with a free hand.

Hicks climbed down, holding the reins. "I need your help, Mary. You know how old Potter was killed—it might be that you know enough to set me on the track of the man that drygulched him."

Mary snorted, winced in pain, and hugged herself a little tighter. "Potter wasn't nothin' to me. Anyhow, dead's dead—nothin' I could say could change that." She disappeared into the tent, then reappeared with a nearly empty whiskey bottle. "I ain't nothin' but a old woman," she whined, "that never hurt nobody in her life. All I want's to be let alone."

"What're you scared of, Mary? I've knowed you, off and on, for a pretty good spell, and I never heard of you turnin' tail to trouble before."

The woman looked at him coldly, then pulled the cork with her teeth and had a go at the bottle. "There ain't nothin' like a mess of busted ribs to convince a-body it's smart to mind his own business."

"The one that beat you up . . . did he give you a guarantee he wouldn't have another thought on the subject, and maybe come back and do the job more permanent?"

Mary's sallow face paled beneath the grime. "Ever'body knows old Mary tends her own business."

"The man that gave you the beatin' wasn't too sure of it."

She started to shrug, then remembered her injury and grunted. "That wasn't the way it was," she said determinedly. "That visit I got . . . well, it was just to kind of remind me that I didn't know nothin'. Just playin' it safe, you might say."

"Playin' it safe." Hicks grinned faintly. "That's what I was sayin'. Sooner or later he'll see there's just one way to

117

play it safe. There's just one kind of folks that don't talk at all. Dead folks."

Mary tensed and took a quick swig from the bottle. "What's the likes of you know about anything?" she demanded. "You're just another sodbuster, like all the others around here. Don't think that star on your vest changes *that*."

The deputy's grin thinned and grew hard. "What if the man that beat you was up at Tribulation right now? What if he was standin' there in front of the general store, or maybe down by the wagon yard? He would of seen me ridin' down here to talk to you—it would have to be you, because the Injuns have all moved back to the reservation. What if he was up there in the street, Mary, lookin' down this way, watchin' us talk like this? How safe do you think he would feel then?"

The woman was visibly shaken. "You're lyin'! He ain't up there!"

Hicks shrugged. "Never said he was."

Mary quickly emptied the bottle and flung it to the ground. She moved out of the tent peering intently at the town. There was a hack and two saddle horses in front of Monday's store. A third saddle animal tied up at the Texas Bar, and a fourth near the cafe. An unusually crowded street, for Tribulation.

There was a man lounging against an awning pole in front of the Square Deal. Being the coolest spot in town, there was almost always someone loafing there. But Mary didn't think of that.

"Who is he?" she asked nervously. "The one in front of Monday's. I can't make him out from here."

"Just a loafer, more'n likely," Hicks said, but his tone was saying something very different.

"What about them saddle animals? You happen to look at any brands before you started down here to plague me?"

Hicks hadn't thought to notice brands—but Mary didn't have to know that. "The hack," he said indifferently, "belongs to a squatter I know. The two horses in front of Monday's is local stock." Hicks hesitated, briefly studied the woman's face, then went on. "The one in front of the cafe wore a brand that I couldn't make out—not from these parts. The roan tied up at the saloon belongs to Pot Allard's Roman Three."

Mary pulled her head in like a turtle. "Git away from me!" she reeled back into the gambling tent and jerked the flap down over the opening. "Git away! Git away!"

For a moment Joe Hicks stared blankly at the hanging flap. He was learning that bounty hunting was not a pleasant profession. Scaring the daylights out of helpless old women kind of went against the grain.

IV

Mary's reaction to the mention of Pot Allard must mean something, but Hicks didn't know just what. One thing he did know, the Durell girl had come into town escorted by an Allard hand. And he had heard stories about Pot himself, and that girl.

Hicks didn't like the way things were adding up. Bess Durell, plus Allard, plus the Grabhorn bounty, plus Shade. And Shade riding alone on Roman Three range. That was the thing that Hicks liked least of all.

The stableman, Ludlow Finch, met Hicks at the wagon yard. "Look here, Deputy, you ain't makin' no friends in Tribulation, shoulderin' up to that troublemaker."

Finch was an easy man not to like, and Hicks didn't try

to hide his feelings. "Troublemaker? I guess you mean Shade."

Hicks picked up his riding gear at the shack and headed for the corral. The stableman shuffled alongside, his face plainly worried. "You know I mean Shade. We want him out of Tribulation, Hicks. We don't like folks meddlin' in our business."

"You stand still for killin'," Hicks said dryly. "And nobody says a thing when an old woman gets whipped nearly to death. But let a pair of strangers ride into Tribulation and ask a few questions . . ."

Finch drew himself up self-righteously. "That old man, Potter—ever'body knowed he was a Injun lover. When you get right down to it, looks like that rifleman done us all a favor by finishin' him off. As for Horseblanket Mary—some Comanche probably caught her dealin' off the bottom."

Hicks grinned coldly. "A Comanche would of knifed her, or maybe stove her head in with a ax—but Injuns don't fight with their hands." The deputy paused at the corral gate and gazed flatly at the stableman. "Me, I'm just a dirt farmer tryin' to make a dollar on the side. I don't know much about troublemakers and killers and women beaters. But I aim to learn, Finch." He raised the barbed-wire loop on the Texas gate. "I aim to learn."

Finch watched worriedly from outside the corral. "Where you headed?" he asked when Hicks was saddled and mounted.

Hicks rubbed his chin thoughtfully. "Now if I was to tell you that, how do I know you wouldn't pass the word along and I'd end up in some dry wash with an ambush bullet in my back?"

Finch's eyes grew wide. "What did Horseblanket Mary tell you!"

Hicks pretended to look worried. "How'd you know . . . ?" Then, apparently catching his mistake, he said, "I mean,

Mary never told me nothin' at all. She's a right stubborn woman." Finch gulped the bait and never knew a hook was in it.

The deputy struck southeast, toward the line camp that served as Roman Three headquarters. He glanced back just in time to see Finch streak up the street and duck into the Texas Bar. He thought grimly, "I hope Mary's got sense enough to look after herself."

He bore south, heading for the cottonwood grove where Shade was supposed to meet the girl. It was beginning to look like the talk to Mary had kicked over a hornet's nest. If it had, Shade would want to know about it fast.

Sure enough, a rider pulled out of Tribulation and disappeared in a wake of dust, heading east. Hicks sighed and wiped his forehead. Finch hadn't wasted any time passing his suspicions to the Roman Three rider, and now the rider was bent on passing them on to Allard.

The deputy's bluff had worked—too well, maybe, as far as Mary was concerned.

V

A few minutes later the deputy found himself not on the road to the cottonwoods, not on the road to anywhere, but lying on his gut on a knoll overlooking the abandoned Indian camp, watching the stir of activity around the gambling lodge.

He looked behind him, at the bottom of the slope where he had staked his animal, and the flat plains beyond. The Roman Three hand was well on his way to the reservation with the news that Horseblanket Mary had been talking again to the deputy sheriff.

Apparently the gambling woman had seen enough to guess at what was happening. First Hicks talking to Finch, then Finch racing to the saloon, and finally that single rider lighting out for the east. As soon as the rider was out of sight, Mary came out of the gambling lodge carrying a blanket roll under one arm. She headed south, directly away from the town.

Hicks watched her stumbling, reeling across the prairie. He shook his head grimly. How far did she expect to get afoot, with no telling how many bruised or busted ribs? "Well," he muttered, "I guess it's just as good I turned back. She *ain't* got sense enough to take care of herself."

There appeared to be no further activity in Tribulation. The town seemed to huddle, dumb and blind, as if trying to persuade itself that its troubles would go away if they were ignored. Hicks backed down the slope, glad to get the town out of his sight.

As soon as Mary came within hailing distance, the deputy shouted, "Over here!"

She stared at him with sickish eyes, breathing raggedly.

"Come on!" he yelled impatiently. "How far can you go afoot, the shape you're in?"

She glanced quickly over her shoulder, at the town. With only the slightest hesitation, she headed toward the deputy. Hicks waited for her behind the knoll, watching her stumble and grunt with pain at every step. Her face was pasty, her breathing came like pop-off steam from a Baldwin engine. The deputy caught her or she would have fallen, then eased her to the ground.

As soon as she could speak, she swore at him. "See what you done! You just wouldn't stay away from me! And now . . ."

"And now," he finished, "you've got Pot Allard at your heels, and that ain't exactly healthy, is it?"

Her gaze sharpened. She hugged herself, moaning, but for the moment she had more than a few splintered ribs to worry about. "I . . . I don't know what you're talkin' about! And I don't think you do, either."

"Sure you do," Hicks said. For the first time since pinning on that star, he was beginning to feel like a peace officer. "It was Allard, or one of his hands, that gave you the beatin', wasn't it?"

She merely glared at him, too out of breath to argue.

"Has to be Allard in back of it," Hicks shrugged. "There wasn't no other rifle in these parts—except the one in the general store, and it don't count. Don't make sense for John Monday to go shootin' people just for the hell of the thing." He shook his head. "It's got to be Allard."

She tried to snort. It was hard to do, with a set of cracked ribs.

"The stableman, Ludlow Finch," Hicks continued, "seems to think it's Allard."

"What . . . what you gettin' at?" The voice was limp and worn out, like the woman.

"When I happened to mention that you'd changed your mind and decided to tell everything you knew, Finch looked like he'd been kicked in the gut. You seen it yourself, didn't you? Finch hot-footed it to the saloon, told one of Allard's hands that Horseblanket Mary had started blabbin' to the county law, and that rider lit out for the Roman Three like his tail was on fire."

"I didn't tell you nothin'!" Those small eyes struck fire.

"Didn't have to. I just told Finch that you did."

Sitting on the ground, Mary pulled herself as erect as possible. "Hicks," she snarled, "you're a fool! You're in as deep as me, and Allard'll squash us both like we was horn fly grubs on one of his prize cows. You don't think the sheriff up at the county seat will do anything about it, do you?" She sneered. "He'll just pin your star on another droughted-out dirt farmer and forget about it. *Then* what good's that bounty money goin' to do you?"

The deputy's eyes widened. "Then Allard *is* Brown?"

Hopelessness moved anger aside and took its place in Mary's face. "I don't know any Brown."

"That's just a name Shade calls him—the express robber that's been dealin' misery to the Grabhorns. Shade figures Allard and Brown is the same."

"I don't know." She was almost beyond caring. "All I know is that folk've got might touchy in these parts. They don't talk about Allard, or his outfit, or the Durells, or anything else he's connected with."

"The Durells?" Hicks frowned.

"Whit Durell's girl, more like it. The one that Pot Allard's got such fancy notions about, so I hear." Once more she tried to snort and was sorry for the effort.

Hicks got back to the main path. "But it *was* one of Allard's hands that gave you the beatin'?"

Mary nodded. What difference did it make now. She was as good as dead, as soon as that rider got his message to Allard. "The gunhand. The one called Handsome Corry."

And Shade, the deputy recalled, was headed for Allard's own back yard, where another bushwhack would be the easiest thing in the world. For a moment Hicks allowed himself to think of that bounty money, all of it his, if something should happen to Shade. If Hicks should capture Brown alone.

But that fantasy lingered only for a moment. The deputy turned to his horse, pulled the stake pin and started to mount.

"What you aim to do about me?" Mary demanded. "I can't go no farther afoot. And I'm good as dead when Pot Allard catches up to me—thanks to you!"

Hicks hesitated, with one foot in the stirrup. Leave her here, he thought. He owed her nothing. If she had talked earlier, Pleasant Potter might be alive right now. She was no good to anybody. If Allard didn't kill her now, the Comanches would later, more than likely, in one of her crooked monte games. So why did he hesitate, when minutes or seconds might mean the difference between life and death for Shade?

"Hicks . . . ?" The woman appeared to read his thoughts, and they scared her. "Hicks, you can't just leave me. . . ."

The deputy groaned. "All right! This old horse will carry double for a little piece, I guess."

CHAPTER NINE

I

SHADE TRAILED THE buckboard at a distance, leading Corry's horse, with the body face down across the saddle. He skirted all timber, staying out of rifle range. He scanned all knolls and high places, watched the horizon for wisps of dust that might indicate approaching horsemen. He had been surprised once today—the next time could be fatal.

As he rode he gave some thought to Bess Durell and her father, to Corry, to Allard, to the town of Tribulation. But he tried not to let his thoughts settle too long on any one person. Until he knew better, he had to think of everyone as his enemy.

He smiled to himself with not the faintest touch of humor. An hour ago he would have found it next to impossible to think of Bess Durell as an enemy. Now he found it amazingly easy.

And what about that new partner of his, that deputy sheriff whose courage came and went, depending on the price of the job? He only had Hicks' word for it that the girl had talked to him. For all he knew, the deputy might be in cahoots with Allard.

And there was White Dog to think about. The Indian had gone to considerable trouble to trail Shade to the cottonwoods. Maybe he had seen things that Shade had missed. It might even be that he had the key to Brown in that silent Indian head of his. But who could get anything out of an Indian? Pleasant Potter, maybe. But he was dead.

Something about that young Kiowa gnawed at Shade. His thoughts drifted to another time, another place. He remembered that there had been little wailing at Potter's burial—but that wasn't quite right. There had been wailing aplenty, but from just one woman, the older woman who had ridden beside the body, holding it in the saddle.

Suddenly Shade knew what it was about White Dog that nagged him. The Kiowa was Pleasant Potter's son!

There was something about the eyes, the carriage, the spread of the shoulders. And the wailing woman was White Dog's mother.

Shade was only mildly surprised. Squaw man, the old scout had been called. This accounted for Potter's leaving all his plunder to White Dog, and it also accounted for the tribal burial, and the killing of Handsome Corry.

Shade's smile was grim. It must have come as a great surprise to Corry—justice in the shape of a young Kiowa warrior suddenly reaching out and touching him like that.

They crossed a small creek that served as the western boundary of the reservation. Fragile dust streamers in the east cut across Shade's meandering thoughts. He nudged the claybank and drew up alongside the buckboard. "Looks like we're gettin' company."

The girl had already seen the dust markers. She looked at Shade with perfect blankness. "Must be Mr. Allard and one of the hands."

She watched him closely. A finger of uneasiness raked up Shade's spine. He was out in the middle of a frozen lake and could hear the ice beginning to crack. The horsemen, two of them, were coming fast. It didn't seem possible that Allard could know so soon about the shooting.

II

Whit Durell was under the brush arbor soaping harness when he saw his daughter in the buckboard start down the long grade toward the soddy. He smiled faintly, a luxury that he didn't often allow himself. He was proud of his daughter. Bess was a good girl, she had a good head on her shoulders, and she was a pleasure to look at. He had never seen a prettier girl—unless it had been her mother. . . .

The smile vanished. His face became a mask.

Now a horseman appeared just behind the buckboard. The mask frowned as Durell recognized Shade's lanky figure. The railroad detective. Bounty hunter, Pot Allard had called him.

The frown deepened. A second rider was following the

man called Shade. No, it wasn't a rider—the animal was following on a lead rope held by Shade. Durell was puzzled. He recognized the horse as the personal animal of Allard's gunhand, Corry. What was Shade doing with it? And why was the railroader trailing after Bess?

Then Durell saw the body. He felt surprise rather than shock. Shade didn't look like the kind of man to outshoot a professional gunman.

The squatter quickly put away the soap and neat's foot. He started toward the sod house at an awkward lope, wiping his hands on the seat of his overalls. An expression of relief cracked Durell's mask when he saw the dust streamers in the east. One thing about Pot Allard—he was a friend you could bank on.

Durell ducked into the soddy. After a moment he reappeared, this time with a rifle.

III

Shade's patience was beginning to wear. He knew that he was nearing that dangerous stage of the hunt that all men come to, sooner or later, when the game is played out too long, when the quarry had become too successful at eluding the hunter. At some uncertain point a peak is reached, and the hunted—if the game is big—suddenly becomes the hunter.

"Well," Shade muttered, "there's not much question about Pot Allard bein' 'big game.'"

Bess Durell looked at him from her seat on the buckboard. There was thoughtfulness in those wide eyes—maybe even a flicker of concern. Suddenly she sat a little straighter and started to speak. At that moment her father appeared in the soddy's doorway, with the rifle, and the words died before they passed her lips.

She had warned Shade once, in a sidelong way, that it would be a serious mistake, and maybe fatal, for him to linger any longer in this country. I guess, Shade thought silently, that kind of bunches me up with the "chosen." The old man didn't get any warnin'. Wonder what makes my case so special?

They had come about halfway down the grade, less than three hundred yards from the soddy, and the riders were not yet in sight. "Miss Durell . . ." Shade spurred in cose to the buckboard. "Looks like there ain't much time, so I won't beat around the bush. I don't know what it is between you and Allard, but I don't figure it can be too much, considerin' Pot's old enough to be your pa."

He blithely ignored her flush of anger. "This here's the way I see it, Miss Durell. This is hard country for squatters —so I don't blame you for makin' a few eyes at Allard and gettin' him to help your pa with the claim. But you don't know what you're lettin' yourself in for."

She stared at him, with spots of color high on her cheeks. She reminded Shade of a spoiled child on the verge of throwing a tantrum. She controled her speech with considerable effort. "What do *you* think I'm lettin' myself in for, Mr. Shade?"

Shade moved his wide whoulders. He didn't have much hope of convincing her. "Well, I guess there ain't any secret about it. I've been on the scout for an express robber— longer than I'd want to admit. But now I've got him pegged. There's enough evidence against Allard to convince most any jury . . ." This wasn't quite true, but those empty cartridge cases at the murder site counted for something. He shook his head for emphasis. "You and your pa are backin' a losin' hand. Nobody can rob an outfit like the Grabhorn Express Company and get away with it forever. . . ."

Far to the east the two horsemen crested a rise, two specks trailed by long streamers of dust.

With no warning at all, Bess Durell suddenly laughed in Shade's ears, there was a chill in the sound of laughter. Maybe the body of Handsome Corry coming on behind had something to do with it. "One of the biggest cattlemen on the reservation! You can't believe that, Mr. Shade."

Shade sighed. "It's more than robbery now. It's murder —an express agent over in the Nations and Pleasant Potter the other night, over in Tribulation."

Those childlike eyes considered him with vague amusement. "Even if it was true, we couldn't help you, Mr. Shade. Mr. Allard is our friend—the best friend we ever had. It ain't likely we'd turn against him."

"Murder," Shade said again, hoping that the word's meaning would get through to her. "He'll be tried for murder, Miss Durell. And likely you and your pa'll stand alongside him as accomplices, unless . . ."

Shade had the unnerving suspicion that he was talking into a vacuum. She smiled blandly and shook her head. "I wouldn't turn against a friend, Mr. Shade. And neither would Pa. Not that Mr. Allard ever done any of these things, of course."

They were within pistol range of the soddy, and Shade had the feeling that Whit Durell, watching his daughter talk so freely with a railroad detective, was far from pleased.

The horsemen were nearing the soddy. With time running out, Shade put his proposition bluntly, in terms that the daughter of a squatter could understand. "There's a considerable price on the killer's head. The Grabhorn bounty . . ."

The wide eyes narrowed slightly. "I've heard."

"Ten thousand dollars it comes to."

She blinked, then frowned, as if trying to imagine what ten thousand dollars might look like. "That much?"

"That much. It could be yours—part of it, anyhow—if you . . ."

She shook her head, but not without obvious regret. "There ain't no way I can help you, Mr. Shade. And," she added, glancing to the east, "it looks like you've waited too long to help yourself."

IV

Shade reined up in front of the soddy, casting uneasy glances into the muzzle of Durell's rifle. "Now," the squatter said tonelessly, "maybe you'd like to do some explainin', mister." He indicated Corry's body with a nod.

Bess Durell looked at Shade, smiled humorlessly. "Mr. Allard will be wanting an explanation too," she said to her father. "I'll be back in a minute."

"What happened to the gunhand?" Durell asked sharply.

"Mr. Shade killed him," the girl said. Some of the wonder was still in her voice. "I'm not sure just how he managed it." She cracked the lines and moved the buckboard around to the side of the house. Shade watched her unhitch with surprising efficiency.

Shade leaned forward in the saddle, hoping to have his say before the horsemen arrived. "Mr. Durell, you know who I am, don't you?"

The rifle didn't waver. The squatter gazed at him, then grunted.

"And you know what I'm doin' here. It's my job to locate the man that's been dealin' misery to the Grabhorn Express Company."

131

"And collectin' the bounty," Durell said sourly, and spat at the ground. "I know who you are, all right."

"The bounty ain't important to me," Shade said. "Not any more. This road agent has already murdered two men that I know about, and no tellin' how many more." The horsemen were now pounding across the flat, less than a thousand yards from the soddy. "I need your help, Durell. All the evidence points to Allard as the express bandit. . . ."

The squatter stared at him, then suddenly spat at the ground. "Mr. Allard will be mighty interested to hear that. Just a minute now, and you can tell him all about it."

Shade rose angrily in his saddle. "Can't you understand what I'm sayin'? Allard's wanted for murder. You and your daughter's settin' yourself up as accomplices, unless . . ."

Shade groaned inwardly. He might as well talk to a fence-post, for all the impression he was making on Durell.

The girl, returning from the horse lot, stood beside her father in front of their soddy. The two riders pulled up in a cloud of reddish dust, dismounted quickly and tied at the rack on the far side of the soddy. Shade recognized Allard's big brown and white pinto. The foreman, Babe Tattersall, rode a roan company gelding with an outsized III on the left shoulder. Shade started to dismount, but Durell said, "Set right where you are, mister. Mr. Allard will tell you when he wants you to get down."

Allard and his foreman tramped across the dooryard, the rowels of their Southwest spurs clamoring. There was an instant, meaningful silence as they paused to gaze at the body of the dead gunman. Shade, realizing that he still had the lead rope in his hand, swore under his breath and let it drop to the ground.

Allard and his foreman continued their heavy march to the soddy's front door. Both men touched hatbrims to Bess Durell. Both looked at the girl in a certain hungry way.

132

But Allard and Tattersall had never had Bess Durell line them up for a bullet in the back. Incidents like that tended to dilute some of the angelic innocence in those wide eyes.

"This here railroader," Whit Durell said to the rancher, "is just full of surprises, ain't he. First he goes and kills a top-notch gunhand, then he starts in to tell me a yarn about . . ."

Allard broke in. "I'd be interested to know how he bested a man like Corry." He gazed unblinkingly at Shade while speaking to Durell. "Where did it happen? And when?"

"Over at the cottonwood grove," Bess said. "Close to the west boundary of your lease. He must have shot Corry from ambush. I didn't see it, but I heard the rifle. When I got there he was standin' over Corry, and your hand was dead."

Allard looked puzzled. "You were in the grove at the time of the killing?"

But what he wanted to know was what had she been doing there alone with Handsome Corry. Bess Durell had understood the unasked question. Confusion tinted her cheeks.

"I guess it wasn't very bright of me, but I thought it would help if I could talk to Mr. Shade . . ."

"How?" Allard asked bluntly.

Shade was doing some fast revising on his first estimate of Allard's toughness. Obviously the rancher was stricken with Bess's youth and beauty, but it had not blinded him. Bess and Handsome Corry—the suspicion was new to Allard, but he didn't reject it simply because it was unpleasant.

"How?" he asked again—not accusingly, but not absently, either. "I don't understand how talkin' to this railroad detective could have helped anyone?"

Now Shade was puzzled. He had assumed that Allard had somehow learned of the shooting on the creek, and that was his reason for streaking in from the reservation. Now it appeared that he had known nothing of the killing.

Shade was wondering what had brought Allard to the Durells' in such a hurry—and so was Bess. Whit Durell's rifle wavered, then strayed slightly to the left. Shade considered his chances. Durell was the only one with a drawn weapon. Maybe, Shade was thinking, he could jump the claybank at Durell, then throw down on the others. Or, if the claybank stirred up enough fuss, maybe he could turn and streak for Tribulation.

It was only a passing thought. So he sat his saddle quietly, mildly folding his hands on the saddle horn. There was a reason for his reluctance to take advantage of Durell's lapse. It might have been a quirk of personality that he had developed in the service of the Choctaw and Canadian Valley Railroad. The truth was, this by-play between Allard and Bess Durell had excited his curiosity. He couldn't bring himself to pick up and leave—even if it had been that easy—without seeing how it came out.

V

At the tender age of six Shade had smoked his first rich black, crooked, rum-cured Conestoga cigar. Since that time he had known beyond a doubt that realization was rarely as sweet as expectation. But it was a natural failing of man to forget the unpleasant and hope for the best. The human animal was a glutton for disappointment.

And Shade was disappointed now. He had expected an unmasking, a display of female temper, or at least a show of indignation on the part of Bess Durell. Instead she smiled,

faintly and a little sadly, at Pot Allard. There was a flush
of color in her cheeks, but the wide-eyed mask remained
firmly in place. Shade found himself wondering if it was
really a mask, after all.

She started to speak, but Allard stopped her with a flick
of his hand. "Babe," he said to his foreman, "you take care
of this railroad man. Take him out back somewheres and
see that he don't stray."

Shade felt cheated. The price of curiosity sometimes came
high—this time it looked as if he might pay with his hide.

Babe Tattersall drew his revolver. "Shuck your pistol,
Shade."

Cautiously, Shade eased his .45 out of his holster and
dropped it. Tattersall motioned for him to get down.

Did he see the glint of amusement in Bess Durell's eyes, or
was it his imagination? Well, it made no difference now.
Shade gazed longingly at his Winchester snugly holstered
in the saddle boot. Then Tattersall gestured with his revolver
and they marched toward the back of the soddy. Whit Durell
followed with a piece of well rope.

"Down on the ground," Tatterall told him. Shade glanced
at Durell, but said nothing. A squatter was not likely to
throw in with a railroad detective against a man like Pot
Allard. He knew what he stood to gain by sticking with Allard—maybe even a rich son-in-law, if he and his daughter
played their cards right. All Shade had to offer was a piece
of the Grabhorn bounty.

Shade followed Tattersall's instructions and stretched out
on the ground. The foreman bound his hands and feet
expertly, as he would hogtie a bawling calf for the branding iron.

For Tattersall, it had been almost too easy. He stood over
Shade, shaking his head slowly, as if pained by the railroader's ineptness. "Mister," he said solemnly, "you ought

135

to of stayed in the Nations. You just haven't caught the hang of doin' things out here on the prairie."

Durell laughed. He stood with both hands plunged into the pockets of his squatter overalls, carelessly cradling the rifle under his right arm. "Babe's right. You never ought to of come. But you can't take back a mistake any more'n you can give back a life—ain't that right, railroader?"

Before Shade could think of an answer, Durell had disappeared around the corner of the soddy, joining his daughter and Allard.

Shade twisted on the ground, making himself as comfortable as possible. Hopefully, he waited for Babe Tattersall to join the powwow with his boss and the Durells. But the foreman merely grinned, hunkered down on his heels and methodically built and lit a smoke.

Shade tried to tune his ears to the buzz of conversation at the front of the house. Then Allard and the Durells moved inside, and there was no chance of hearing anything through the foot-thick walls of the soddy. Shade turned his attention to the foreman.

For the best part of a minute Tattersall had been staring at him with a puzzled expression. "You're a hard one to peg," he said finally. "I've been studyin' on it, lookin' at it on all sides, and it just don't figure for you to outshoot a hired gun like Handsome Corry. How'd you manage it?"

Shade's grin was a bit sour, but it was a grin. "Maybe you folks underestimate me. Maybe your gunhand got careless. Or maybe I had help."

Tattersall considered the possibilities one at a time, and discarded them. "Nope," he said soberly, "back in the States you might be all right. Or even in the Nations. Back where the gents wear button-up shoes and plug hats and carry them little double action .38s around in their hip pockets. Here it's different."

Clearly, the foreman didn't believe that Shade had been underestimated. "And Corry didn't make a mistake. He knew his business."

"In his business, one mistake's all that's needed."

But Tattersall wouldn't have it. "No, it was somethin' else. As for you havin' help—well, Bess was there, and she didn't see anybody. Just you."

Shade squinted thoughtfully. "Did you ever think that it might of been Bess herself that gave me the help?"

Strangely, Tattersall didn't dismiss the notion immediately, as Shade had expected. "Why would a girl like Bess want to throw in with you?"

Shade was feeling his way blindly. "Maybe Bess was tired havin' a gunhand trailin' her wherever she went . . ." This kind of "thinking out loud" led off in several directions, but Shade kept to the main path. The fact that Tattersall hadn't rejected the idea must mean something.

He continued. "A girl like Bess—young, plenty easy to look at, full of vinegar—you can't really blame her, can you? Bad enough she's saddled to a man twice her age, just because her pa needs Allard's help." He was moving cautiously, half-expecting a show of anger or indignation. But the foreman showed only a worried interest.

Tattersall broke the moment of silence. "Just what is it you're tryin' to say?"

Shade tried to shrug, but only pulled the knots tighter about his ankles and wrists. "You've got eyes, Tattersall. You can see how it is with your boss and Bess Durell. Tell me somethin'—why did Allard hire Corry in the first place? To fight rustlers, or to scare off Bess Durell's other suitors?"

Tattersall looked at him for what seemed a long time. "No sir," he said softly, "you never should of left the Nations."

137

"Does that mean that Allard aims to kill me?" The words sounded much less concerned than he felt.

"How would I know what Pot Allard aims to do? I just work for him."

The foreman sounded a little sour. Good. Shade hoped to get them scrapping among themselves. "Like you say, you work for him. Does that include doin' his killin' for him?"

"Not for Pot Allard. . . ." The foreman pulled up short, realizing that he was doing too much talking. He snapped away the dead stub of his cigarette and began building a new one.

"Was it you that killed Pleasant Potter, Tattersall?"

Tattersall snorted and licked his smoke.

"Was it Corry, on Allard's orders, or maybe Allard himself?"

The foreman clamped his heavy jaw and said nothing. Shade thought angrily, "If I get killed, at least I want to know who to cuss for it." He had to get Tattersall to talking again—and that meant stirring him up.

Shade surprised the foreman by laughing in his face. "Tattersall, you're a fool. You moon around Bess Durell like a lovesick calf, but you haven't got the gall to take your own part when you're around her. You let yourself be buffaloed by your boss, like his word was the gospel. You let a tinhorn killer trail after Bess like a pet coon, and you don't do a thing to stop it. What kind of a hold has Allard got on you, anyhow?"

"Shut up," Tattersall said softly.

But the time for shutting up had passed. "And how about me," Shade pressed. "A railroad detective goes skippin' off to a cottonwood grove with your darlin' Bess, and you still do nothin'. One thing about Handsome Corry—he *tried*."

Tattersall came to his feet. "I told you to shut up!"

Shade tried to grin. It wasn't easy, with his arms and legs growing numb from the tightened knots. "Tattersall, you're a bigger fool than you know. You could be a rich man. Did you know that? Did you know there's a ten thousand dollar bounty on Allard's head?"

How many times, Shade wondered, had he already promised that bounty away? If he split it up as many times as he had promised, there wouldn't be enough left to pay for a bundle of New Orleans cigars.

"Money," he went on doggedly, trying not to see the thunder in the big foreman's face. "Money's the thing that counts with girls like Bess . . ."

Well, Shade remembered thinking, I wanted to stir him up. And I've done *that*, all right!

It was the last conscious thought to enter his head before Tattersall suddenly grabbed him by his shirtfront, jerked him half off the ground and exploded a big fist alongside Shade's left ear.

CHAPTER TEN

I

THE HORIZON tilted sickeningly, then settled with a shudder. Down in the bottom a section of the grubby corn swayed crazily. Shade blinked and tried to clear his head. There was no wind—but the corn stalks were swaying.

139

He closed his eyes. Through the pounding in his head he heard Babe Tattersall saying, "No need to worry about him givin' us any trouble now."

Whit Durell laughed. It wasn't a pleasant sound. Then Pot Allard said in a strangely worried voice, "He looks dead to me."

"He ain't dead." Shade slitted one eye and brought the fuzzy figures into focus. Tattersall and his boss and the squatter were standing near the corner of the soddy, watching him thoughtfully. Durell and Allard, Shade reasoned, must have heard the fuss and come out to see what was going on. Bess Durell stepped in front of the men and silently gazed at the trussed-up figure at her feet. There was a certain calculating light in those childlike eyes that Shade didn't understand. And what he didn't understand he didn't like.

Just before he closed the slitted eye, Shade saw her smile, very faintly. That did nothing to improve his peace of mind.

"Somebody ought to watch him," Allard said: "Just in case."

"In case of what?" Tattersall asked dryly. "He can't get out of them ropes. And if he hollers, who would hear him? For that matter, if he was to die, who would care?"

"I would," Allard said grimly. "The Grabhorns run a powerful outfit. The more of their agents that get killed, the tougher they're goin' to be." Suddenly his voice was taut with anger. "That fool, Corry! Bess, what made you put him up to such a thing!"

Shade lay perfectly still. He could imagine Bess staring at Allard with that hurt, wide-eyed look, as if he had slapped her. "What else could I do? Shade was askin' all kinds of questions. It was all over Tribulation. Folks was beginnin' to take interest. Why, if a railroader and a deputy sheriff could poke in our business without gettin' hurt, a lot of others in Tribulation might get the same idea."

Allard made a sound deep in his chest; it was almost a groan. "I didn't aim to bark at you, Bess. You're right. Horseblanket Mary has already started talkin' to the deputy, accordin' to one of my hands that just come back from town."

A light turned on in Shade's mind. So it hadn't been Corry's killing that had brought Allard running, after all. The gambling woman had started talking to Hicks—it was almost more than Shade could believe.

"I don't like this," Whit Durell said nervously. "You right sure about Mary and that deputy?"

"Ludlow Finch was sure, and he told my rider, and my rider told me. That's all I know. I'm sorry you don't like it, Durell. That's too goddamn bad."

Bess Durell said mildly, as though her mind were somewhere else, "Don't talk to my pa like that, Mr. Allard."

Shade could hear the cowman gulping his anger. "No offense, Whit," he said stiffly.

The squatter shuffled. "None taken, Mr. Allard."

"All this ain't doin' none of us a bit of good," Babe Tattersall blurted, "standin' here beggin' one another's pardon. We all know what's got to be done. Bess had the right idea about this railroader—it ain't her fault if Corry bungled the job."

Whit Durell sounded alarmed. "You can't kill the railroader—not here on my property!"

Pot Allard sighed loudly. "We don't aim to kill him here. If it has to be done, we'll take him out somewheres. It just come to me that if we was to make it look like the railroader and the deputy had a fallin' out . . ."

The squatter and Tattersall got the idea immediately, "Maybe they fell out over the way to split up the bounty,"

Durell said. Tattersall laughed harshly. "So they kill each other in a gunfight. But that still leaves Horseblanket Mary."

"Mary ain't nothin' to trouble about," the big foreman said. "She can't run far, with them busted ribs."

There was a moment of chill silence as the four of them considered murder. Shade lay as still as the dead, a sickish feeling in his gut.

"We better talk this over some," Pot Allard said at last. "Bess, would you make us some coffee?"

"There's some in the pot, on the back lid," she said absently. Shade could almost feel her looking at him, studying him, sizing him up. "You men go on in the house and talk—I'll watch the railroader for you."

Shade heard the men tramp back to the soddy. The beaded sweat on his forehead was as cold as frost on a yellow slicker. There was electricity in the silence.

Then Bess Durell said, "All right, Mr. Railroad Man, you don't have to go on playin' possum on my account."

II

"Mr. Shade . . ." The girl knelt beside him, speaking softly. "Mr. Shade, you ain't really hurt, are you?"

Shade stared at her amazed, as always, by her beauty— even when he knew it was only a shell. "I'll live," he said huskily. "Leastwise, till you and your menfolks decide on a fit way to murder me."

Her cheeks flushed. The wide eyes looked pained. "Don't you understand, I want to help you!"

Shade squinted. "Why?"

"I . . . I . . . see how wrong it is now, the things Mr.

Allard made us do. I want to do something to help make up for all that . . ."

But Shade noticed that she was making no effort to untie his ropes. "Are you tellin' me that Allard is Brown?" She looked blank, and he added. "The shotgunner that took such a fancy to Grabhorn Express carriers."

She nodded quickly. "Yes, Mr. Allard is the one."

"Can you prove it? In court, I mean. Could you produce solid evidence to prove Allard's actually the man I'm lookin' for?"

"Yes, I'm sure I could." She nodded again, eagerly, and Shade had no doubt that, as a witness for the prosecution, Bess Durell would have little difficulty convincing a frontier jury. But she still hadn't touched those ropes.

"If you've got a knife," he started, "or if you could untie these knots . . ."

She almost smiled. "There's somethin'," she said slowly, "that we ought to get straight."

Shade knew what was coming. "You want a cut of the bounty money," he said tonelessly.

"Not a cut, Mr. Shade." This time she did smile. "I want it all. Every dollar. And I'll want you to write a letter to the express company, tellin' them that catchin' the robber is all my doin', and all the money goes to me."

Men, it occurred to Shade, were too trusting. Pleasant Potter and Joe Hicks had been satisfied to take his word on the division of the reward money, when and if they got it. But not this girl with the childlike face and the innocent eyes.

"I've seen Osage horse traders," he said wryly, "that drove easier bargains. But you don't leave me much choice."

"Live or die, Mr. Shade." She shrugged. "That's your choice."

Suddenly, as though a mask had been removed, she was

no longer beautiful. No longer innocent. And certainly not helpless. He stared so hard and long that she scowled. He decided that he liked her scowl better than her smile.

She said impatiently, "There ain't much time. The menfolks won't stay in the house forever."

The wise man, Shade tried to tell himself, knows when he's had the worst of it. "It's a bargain. Now, if you'll cut these ropes."

"First things first," she said mysteriously.

Shade watched her rise and walk unhurriedly toward the house. She disappeared around the corner of the soddy. Shade's hope lay cold in the bottom of his belly. Had she been teasing him, laughing at him all the time?

She appeared again, rounding the rear of the soddy. Dry mouthed, Shade said, "Look here, if this is some kind of game . . ."

"It ain't a game, Mr. Shade," she said calmly. "It's deadly serious. Mr. Allard's in there right now, him and Babe Tattersall, figurin' out a way to kill you and the deputy and that old gamblin' woman."

"And your pa?" The taste of gall was in Shade's mouth. "What's he doin' about it?"

In one hand she carred a curved sickle with a glistening edge, in the other she had a piece of tablet paper and a pencil stub. "Nothin' Pa *can* do," she shrugged, kneeling again at Shade's side. "We're just squatters—we have to do whatever men like Mr. Allard tells us."

"Includin' murder?"

But her face had gone blank again. "Don't make me sorry for tryin' to help you, Mr. Shade. Roll over on your front side, so I can get at the rope."

Shade did as she directed. Sun-warmed steel slipped between his wrists and quickly sliced through the hemp knots. Shade rolled over again and pushed himself to a sitting position. The girl moved quickly. As he rubbed feeling into his numb hands she slipped behind him. Too late Shade realized what she was up to. He glimpsed the point of the sickle slant down from behind his right shoulder, then the bright, keen edge of steel touched his throat.

"Don't move," she told him, "except to do what I tell you."

Shade sat rigidly. The blade lay steadily on his throat, just above the Adam's apple, next to the great artery in the side of his neck.

"Take this," Bess said, passing the pencil and paper to him with her left hand. "Write that letter to the express folks —the one tellin' about the bounty belongin' to me."

Thoughts crowded Shade's head. A letter was just a letter. When this thing was over, and if he actually did return with Brown's scalp flying from his lance head, he could tell the straight of it in his report.

Like hell he could. A snip of a girl, first tricking him into an attempted bushwhack, then beating him out of the bounty —they would laugh him right out of the Division office. Turn in a story like that and the company wouldn't take him back as a section hand. He knew it, and the girl knew it.

Cautiously, Shade reached for the paper. Bess eased her pressure on the blade, but not by much.

Awkwardly, Shade pulled up his bound feet and smoothed the paper on his knee. "All right." His voice came out as a muffled snarl. "What do you want me to write?"

There was a moment of indecision. Maybe, Shade thought, she can't even read. But it was nothing he wanted to bank on. At last she said, "Just write it, what I told you. I'll let you know if it don't sound right."

The was something about the touch of steel against his throat that encouraged cooperation. Shade began the message in the slow, careful hand of a self-taught penman. He addressed it to his box at the Division office. *I, Frank Shade, special agent of the Choctaw and Canadian Valley Railroad, do recommend that the bearer of this note, Bess Durell, be awarded all monies and rewards offered for the capture of the person responsible for the several robberies and other violent crimes against the C & CVRR and the Grabhorn Express Company.*

"Ain't you bein' just a mite fancy?" she asked suspiciously.

"I can change it. If that's what you want."

She considered it briefly and decided to let it stand. "Now put it in there that I get all the bounty, and don't have to split it with anybody."

He wrote it in, then signed his name. "Now, if you'll just let up on that sickle."

The threat of steel was removed as Bess took the note and read it slowly, word by word. "Of course," Shade said, cutting his feet free, "that note don't mean a thing unless I bring Allard in and can prove he's the one I'm after."

"He's the one," she said flatly. "And there'll be proof . . . when the time comes."

Shade glared. "The time's now. He's right there in the house, not suspectin' a thing. Ain't likely I'll ever get a better chance to take him without gettin' myself shot."

But Bess Durell was stubbornly shaking her head. "It can't be risked. Babe Tattersall's temper's on a short fuse—there'd be a fight and my pa might get hurt. Besides, I ain't right sure yet about that proof against Mr. Allard."

Shade was keenly aware of the passing seconds. Time could easily be his life, growing shorter than he knew. If Allard or his foreman should come out of the house unexpectedly . . . "At least," he said grudgingly, "I've got to have a horse. None of this is goin' to do any good if I'm left afoot."

She was looking at him in a certain way that made his

146

scalp prickle. He was beginning to know Miss Bess Durell. This, he thought to himself, is probably the way she will look at Allard, just before the hangman kicks the trap out from under him. At that moment Shade could almost feel sorry for Pot Allard. He knew about cattle, and he had been a great success as a robber of express carriers, but he had a lot to learn about women.

"If you're thinkin' about killin' me," Shade said quietly, "put it out of your mind. That note won't mean much without I'm on hand to vouch for it. There's too many others that's got their claims in for that bounty."

She blinked, only mildly surprised that he had read her thoughts. "Maybe," she shrugged. "Maybe not. Anyhow, it's not important." She didn't want to overplay her hand and risk losing everything. "The important thing is the deputy sheriff that's been hidin' down there in the corn patch."

Startled, Shade stared at the patch of grubby corn in the bottom near the creek. He remembered seeing those dry stalks moving in the still afternoon, and wondering about it. "How do you know it's the deputy?"

"I seen him ridin' through the cottonwoods just before Babe Tattersall hit you. He crossed the creek and crawled into the bottom corn—the menfolks was too busy to notice."

Shade stared at her. That innocent, wide-eyed look would never seem real again. "I guess you had a reason for not givin' the deputy away."

"Two reasons. If he'd started shootin', he might of hit my pa. Also, he couldn't of slipped up here to the soddy while I was busy inside gettin' the pencil and paper. And he couldn't of waited for me at the back of the house, and then hit me over the head with somethin' so that it would be maybe five minutes before I came to my senses and begin yellin' that the deputy had cut you loose and got away."

It took Shade a moment to understand. Then he said with

awe, "That's some scheme. But it still doesn't get me a horse or a gun."

"You'll have to rustle horses and guns for yourself. All I can give you is five minutes' time, and maybe send Mr. Allard off in another direction to look for you."

Shade looked down at his right hand. It was already a fist. "I guess you aim for me to do the hittin'. It'll have to be the real thing, if you aim to make Allard believe your story."

She flashed a chilling smile. "I've been knocked around some. I can take it. Don't you go chicken-gutted on my account, and make a mess of things." Almost as an afterthought, she said, "You know of a place called Hard Fork?"

". . . I don't think so."

"It's not far, the deputy will know where. Wait there. I'll bring you the proof you want, and the man to go with it." A brief silence followed her words. "Well!" she hissed, "what are you waitin' on!"

Shade half-raised his hand, then hesitated. The top of her head just reached to his shoulders. She looked very small and fragile—but then, so did a cottonmouth snake when it was half grown and at its deadliest.

When it was over, Shade stared for a moment at his fist. He had never hit a woman before. He had never imagined that it could be so easy.

CHAPTER ELEVEN

I

DEPUTY JOE HICKS lay between furrows, watching the strange scene over the sights of his rifle. He was heartily relieved when the girl cut Shade free of his ropes. Hicks had been trying for several minutes to persuade himself to go to Shade's rescue and somehow, in the process, put Allard under arrest. It was an unpleasant and suicidal notion any way he looked at it.

Then the girl had cut Shade free, and the deputy's sense of duty was never put to the test. His conscience was clear. Thanks to the girl, he had held to that fragile and most essential fraction of a man, his self-respect.

He could hardly believe his eyes when Shade suddenly, and for no apparent reason, struck the girl a savage blow that sent her reeling for more than a dozen yards before she collapsed near the Durell soddy. In a righteous rage, Hicks lined Shade's fleeing figure in his sights. The deputy choked with indignation. His finger tensed on the trigger. Any man who would strike a woman—especially a woman who had just befriended him—deserved to be shot.

But his finger eased on the trigger. Something queer was happening—now that he thought about it, everything about the scene rang slightly false.

Shade, with all the gangling awkwardness of a long-time horseman, was coming directly at the deputy at a jarring gallop. It seemed to the deputy that he was trying to run right down the barrel of his rifle. Scowling, Hicks lowered the muzzle. Shade gestured urgently, all the time wheezing and blowing and pumping his arms, mouthing words that the deputy couldn't make out.

It was obvious that Shade had known that he was in the corn field. Slowly, Hicks stood up among the brown stalks as the railroader charged down the long grade.

Shade pulled up beside the deputy, gasping for breath. Between great gulps of air, he demanded, "Where's your horse at?"

But Hicks' thoughts were somewhere else. "I seen what you done to that girl! I'll tell you somethin', Shade—I never would of tied up with you if I'd of knowed . . ."

"The horse!" Shade gasped impatiently.

But the deputy clung to his thought like a pit bull with a bone. ". . . If I'd of knowed what kind of man you was! Beatin' on womenfolks is somethin' I never took a likin' to." His scowl darkened. "Somethin' comes to me. Maybe it was *you* that done that thing to Horseblanket Mary."

Shade's anger suddenly boiled over. He knocked the deputy's rifle to one side and grabbed him in a beartrap grip. "I ain't got time to listen to a sermon!" he snarled. "So shut up and tell me what you done with your horse."

There was something in Shade's voice, if not his words— a certain glint in those angry eyes—that caused Hicks to stop babbling. This was not the grim but inept Frank Shade that Hicks had known only a few hours ago. He was stronger, tougher, angrier. This Frank Shade, as the deputy sized him up, was not a man it would pay to dally with.

"The horse," Hicks said, struggling to free himself from the steely grip, "is down the creek a piece."

Shade turned him loose and gave him a shove toward the creek. "Where's *your* animal?" Hicks demanded, stumbling between the rows of corn, at Shade's prodding.

"Back at the Durell place, along with my guns, and some of my skin." He rubbed the raw place on his jaw where Tattersall had slugged him.

They reached the rear bank of the stream, an abrupt drop of about six feet to the sloping bed and trickle of water. The deputy's horse dozed near the edge of the water, at the end of a stake rope. Hicks was getting set to descend the steep bank when Shade took his arm. "Hold on a minute. I want to see just how far we can trust the Durell girl."

Hicks glared at him. "It ain't likely she'll put much trust in *you.*"

There was a kind of secret savagery in Shade's grin, but he made no effort to explain his actions. He had to backtrack through more cottonwoods before he could see what was happening at the soddy.

Apparently Bess Durell was just recovering from her contact with Shade's fist. Shade could see her kneeling, shaking her head, as if trying to clear it. "I guess she ain't started yellin' yet," Shade thought aloud.

"I mean it," the outraged deputy said bitterly, "if I'd of knowed . . ."

"Shut up," Shade told him, "and give me your rifle." He took the rifle out of Hicks' surprised hands. "If she turns on me now, I don't want to be caught naked against a shotgunner." He frowned. "That's kind of funny, now that I think about it."

Hicks looked his silent disgust, which Shade ignored. "I mean," he continued, still thinking aloud, "the gent that's at the bottom of all this—the only weapon anybody ever seen him with is a scatter-gun. It's the reason we called him

151

Brown, in the first place. Somewhere along the line I got switched off to Henry rifles. . . ."

The thought was shunted to a sidetrack to be picked up later. Bess Durell was getting to her feet. She looked first in the direction of the creek, then turned slowly, scanning the prairie in all directions. Shade was forced to admire her for the amazing toughness that lay beneath that childlike exterior. She hadn't even lifted a hand to touch the place where the blow had landed. Shade had known his share of hardcased—they came in all degrees of toughness—but he had never seen one quite that indifferent to pain.

The quiet drama at the top of the slope had finally caught the deputy's attention. "What's she doin'?"

Shade grinned thinly. "Makin' sure I got out of sight before she starts makin' a fuss about you knockin' her over the head and cuttin' me loose."

Hicks looked startled. "*Me* knockin' her over the head!"

With a certain perverse pleasure, Shade briefly explained the scheme as Bess Durell had thought it up. The deputy paled. "Pot Allard would kill me without battin' an eye, if he thought I ever did a thing like that!"

"He'll kill you anyhow, if he finds you. You, and me, and Horseblanket Mary."

Joe Hicks looked as if he might be sick. Up on the slope, Bess Durell was raising the curtain on the next act. She called shrilly, and Allard and Durell and Tattersall dashed out of the soddy almost before the sound reached as far as the creek. The men crowded around the girl. It was easy for Shade to imagine the outrage that must be turning the air blue in the vicinity of the Durell soddy.

"What will happen now?" Hicks asked nervously.

"I hope the girl will tell them we headed upstream, and that Allard will believe her."

"What if he don't?"

"That's somethin' I'd rather not think about. How's that horse of yours for carryin' double?"

The question did nothing to settle the deputy's nerves. "The animal's already done its part of carryin' double today. On my account, Horseblanket Mary figures Allard aims to kill her. I had to bring her part way from Tribulation— I left her under a rock shelf in the creek bed, about a mile downstream."

Shade groaned. Having a wounded gambling woman on his hands wasn't going to make things any easier. Still, he guessed that Mary had a right to lay some of her trouble at his door.

Up on the slope Allard and his foreman were running for their horses. Whit Durell was staying at the soddy with his daughter. "Won't be long now," Shade thought to himself. "We'll soon know what side Miss Durell has finally decided to line up with."

He breathed a deep sigh of relief when Allard and Tattersall streaked almost due north toward the upper reaches of the stream. "There's a place called Hard Fork not far from here," he said. "You know where it is?"

Hicks gazed bleakly at the retreating figures of the horsemen. He didn't seem particularly pleased that Bess Durell had not betrayed them. "Hard Fork? It's over to the east, in the reservation."

Shade would have liked it better if it hadn't been in Allard's back yard, but he was in a poor position to complain. In any case, they couldn't risk striking for the reservation before nightfall. He said reluctantly, "We might as well see if we can find the gamblin' woman."

THE GRABHORN BOUNTY

II

Horseblanket Mary huddled beneath the jutting sandstone outcrop cursing the day that Frank Shade had shown his face in Tribulation. Until that time living had been relatively easy. Plenty of Comanches eager to get themselves fleeced out of their grass money. A quiet little town to live in, where folks minded their own business. No local law. No worries at all to speak of. Live and let live. If now and then there were rumors of queer doings over at the Roman Three, nobody cared. If Pot Allard wanted to take in after a squatter girl, that was his affair. If he favored turning a few dollars outside the cattle business, that also was Pot's affair.

Everything quiet and peaceful.

"Now look at it!" the woman muttered to herself. "An old man gets shot right out of his bed at night. An old woman gets her ribs stove in. All of a sudden ever'body's scared to look his neighbor in the eye. Afraid to set foot in the street, pert nigh, without Pot Allard says it's all right!"

She grunted disgustedly, gazing bleakly at the stand of cottonwood and walnut on the far bank, and the lacy green willows near the water. Everything was crazy. The whole world, it seemed, had lost its mind. All because a no-good railroad agent . . .

Not that Mary actually believed that Shade was the real cause of their grief. It was just something that she, like the others in Tribulation, told herself to keep from wondering too much about the truth. Oh, there had been whispers, but nobody had listened. Not even to rumors of bounty. Money was fine—nobody in Tribulation had anything against money —but staying alive was better.

154

THE GRABHORN BOUNTY

It was said that when a man turned Pot Allard against him, his chances for a long life grew noticeably shorter. Mary had reason to believe it.

But the queerest thing of all, the frightening thing, and the hardest to understand, was that Pot Allard had once been as straight as a ramrod and there was hardly a person in the county that hadn't been his friend.

Well, times change. Men change—and usually it's women that do the changing.

Mary brooded over that philosophy for some time. She had never trusted that little snip of a squatter girl. A sugar-sweet smile and a pretty face made fools of men, but Mary had never been taken in. A girl like that didn't set her sights on a man in his fifties unless . . .

She heard a horse plodding downstream in the shallow water.

"Mary," the deputy called, "it's me, Joe Hicks."

The woman gained her feet with much grunting and waddled to the rim of the overhand. "Where you been?" she demanded. "You been gone long enough. Did you bring any grub?"

"No grub." The deputy tied his weary animal in some salt cedar beneath the shelf. "Just the railroader."

Mary scowled, seeing nothing of a second rider. Hicks scaled the claybank and wiped his sweaty face with his hand. "Shade had to leave his horse behind, his guns too. That animal of mine's about played out. Shade's comin' on afoot—said he wanted to scout the east bank."

As briefly as possible he told Mary about what he had seen and what Shade had told him. The woman pursed her lips as if to whistle. "So it's Pot Allard that's been robbin' them express cars!"

Hicks shrugged. "Not much doubt about it now." But something was worrying him. "It don't make much sense,

155

does it? Pot Allard—why would a man like that want to turn road agent?"

Mary made a cackling sound that might have been laugher. "I figure Pot never had anything to say about it. Looks like the cattle business just wasn't enough to satisfy that squatter girl."

Shade appeared suddenly at the edge of the overhang. He swung quickly beneath the jutting rock, whipping his rifle—the deputy's rifle—around so that the muzzle was almost against the buckle of Hicks' gun belt. The deputy made a startled sound. Mary blinked, scowled, and quickly decided that she didn't like what she saw in the railroader's eyes.

"Look here!" Hicks blustered, inching away from the gun. "What do you think . . ."

"What if I had been Pot Allard?" Shade asked flatly. "Two twitches of the trigger finger and two thirds of his trouble would be over."

"Hell," Hicks said, recoving from his scare. "Allard ain't nowhere near here. We both saw him and Tattersall head the other way."

Shade groaned to himself. He was about to explain that horses could be turned around, then decided that it would be a waste of breath. He turned to the woman. "You was sayin' somethin' about the squatter girl?"

Mary blinked again, nervously. "It wasn't nothin'. It just come to me, kind of, that two winters back we had a big die-up. One of them fast northers whistlin' down from Kansas. Lot of cows piled up against snow fences and froze. The big damage was over to the west, we heard, above the Cap Rock. But maybe Allard got hurt worse than any of us knowed."

Shade nodded slowly. It was the most sensible reason he had heard yet for a well-known rancher to take up express robbing. A little push from Bess Durell might have done it —if he actually was running a bankrupt brand.

The woman muttered something under her breath, then spat at the ground. "I've seen her kind before. Sweet as 'lasses candy when she wants to be. Helpless as a crippled calf in a flash flood. But all the time she's got a razor up her sleeve, ready to cut your gizzard out the first time you bat your eyes."

Shade grinned faintly. "But if our necks are goin' to get saved, she's the one that's got to save them."

Horseblanket Mary stared at him and spat again. "Men! You're like all the others—bait you with a pretty face and you ain't got the sense of a musk hog." Somewhere behind that puffy face a shrewd brain was working. "If Pot Allard can't trust the Durell girl," she said sharply, "how do you figure *you* can?"

The answer came to Joe Hicks immediately. "The bounty money." He glared at Shade. "You promised her the bounty money, didn't you?"

"Now look here," Horseblanket Mary flared. "I got a right to some of that bounty! Look at me—a old woman so stove up she can't hardly breath. All on your account, railroader."

"What about *me?*" the deputy said indignantly. "You promised I'd get a full share, Shade. You can't get around *that!*"

Shade stared at the two of them with a coldness that caused them to look away. "Maybe we ought to catch our man before we start cuttin' up the bounty."

III

Taking turns, the men stood watch in a dense growth of mullein above the overhang. The bounty discussion had been dropped. But not the thinking.

"I been thinkin'," Mary said once, peering at Shade with those shoe-button eyes. "You workin' for the railroad, like you do, makes me wonder . . ."

Shade grinned, this time with feeling. "There's no strings to the Grabhorn offer. The one that brings in Brown collects the money."

A watery smile tugged at the woman's lax mouth. "You wouldn't go and do a old woman out of what's rightly hers, would you, Shade?"

Shade had ejected all the ammunition in Hicks' rifle and was carefully cleaning each cartridge before pressing it back into the magazine. Hicks was up in the mullein patch keeping watch, Shade hoped, for sign of Allard and the foreman. "How much you figure is rightly yours?"

"Well . . ." The gleam of greed was in those eyes. "Share and share alike, that's good enough for me. Old Mary don't want more'n anybody else. Fair's fair. Split 'er up three ways," she said generously, "between me and you and Hicks."

"Three ways . . ." Shade put the last cartridge in the rifle and tried the action. "What about Bess Durell?"

She started to swell up with indignation, but something in Shade's voice caused her to consider. "You figure she's got a right to that money?" she asked cautiously.

"Nobody's got a right yet. We ain't got our hands on Brown."

158

THE GRABHORN BOUNTY

"But when we do?" Mary was getting worried.

"When we do, and if we do, it will be mostly the doin' of Bess Durell."

The gambling woman could see that a change in tactics was called for. "Listen to me," she said in a soothing, motherly tone. "I tell you I know more about Bess Durell than you do. Sure, she's got looks, and she's got somethin' else, a way about her that makes men think they just *got* to look after her. But she's a fake, Shade. Fake as that fool's gold up in the Wichitas that greenhorns load theirselves down with." She shook her head in obvious irritation. "I don't know why I bother with you. Men never listen to anybody when they talk against girls like that."

"Then," Shade asked dryly, "why *do* you bother?"

She glared and pointedly ignored the question. "But I aim to tell you, anyhow, even if you don't listen. Right now she's just a squatter girl with a fool of a gray-headed cowman on her line. But she won't be a squatter girl for long. I've seen her likes before—fancy little snips with notions inside their curly heads that would make a man's blood run cold. Shade, how'd you like to see your untouched little squatter girl five years from now? All you got to do is catch on with a trail herd and strike for Dodge or some other cowtown. Or maybe a minin' camp. Or an end-of-track shanty town."

Shade glanced at her sharply, but she didn't seem to notice. "There you'll find your Miss Durell in some saloon, or dance hall, or gamblin' shack fleecin' the short horns with both hands. And when you see her there, don't you feel sorry for her, because right there's where she belongs and where she wants to be. And when, some night, you happen to cross down below the deadline and see her again, only older and fatter, in one of the cribs on the east side of the tracks, well don't feel sorry for her then, either . . ."

Shade stared at her. For just a moment he had glimpsed

a Mary that few people knew existed, the woman who had been hiding for the Lord knew how long behind a puffy face and layers of fat.

"This squatter girl," he said at last. "Bess Durell. How come you know so much about her?"

Seconds passed in uneasy silence. Mary turned and stared out at the glistening trees on the far bank. "You wouldn't think it to look at me now," she said at last, "but I was a Bess Durell once myself."

Shade waited a moment, then decided there was nothing more to be said. He climbed the bank and spelled Hicks in the mullein patch.

CHAPTER TWELVE

I

TOWARD SUNDOWN Shade, hunkering in the tall weeds, heard the beat of distant hoofs. He had expected Allard to gather his Roman Three hands and start a systematic search when he and Tattersall failed to pick up Shade's trail. But so soon?

Hicks appeared over the rim of the creekbank. "What's happenin' up here?" The deputy was frankly worried.

"I don't know." Shade jacked a cartridge into the chamber of the rifle. "But I aim to find out." He moved cautiously

to the edge of the brush until he saw the two riders driving
a small band of horses to the east. The horsebackers rode
on blanket pads, Plains Indian fashion. Both men wore Army
shirts, full-length leggings, and breechclouts.

Hicks, who had come up behind Shade, said, "What outfit do you make them?"

"Kiowa or Comanche—I don't know. Get Mary up here."

"The way she's stove up?"

"Get her up here." Shade left no space for argument. He
waited impatiently at the edge of the brush, watching the
Indian mustangers or horse traders, or horse thieves—he
didn't know which and didn't particularly care. In a few
minutes Hicks reappeared over the lip of the bank and came
toward Shade, dragging Horseblanket Mary through the
patch of mullein.

"How do you make them?" Shade asked. "Kiowa or Comanche?"

Wheezing and grunting and muttering under her breath,
Mary glanced briefly at the horsemen. "Kiowa, of course,"
she said disgustedly. "Look at the heel tassels."

"You sure?"

She peered at him through folds of fat. "I can see the
medicine dance scars right through them Army shirts. What
difference does it make?"

"Maybe none . . ." He hesitated only an instant, then
wheeled and raced back through the brush. Startled, Mary
and the deputy watched him drop over the edge of the bank
and scramble down the steep incline. Seconds later they
glimpsed the deputy's tired animal pounding downstream,
with Shade in the saddle.

"Well!" Mary snorted. "What do you think about that?"

The deputy shook his head worriedly.

The Indians unhurriedly moved the pony herd toward
the reservation. As Shade rode toward them, the Indians

closed in quietly on the flanks of their herd, bunching them, easing them almost to a standstill.

One Kiowa was old, very wrinkled and dark. The other was younger than Shade, his wide, Kiowa face glowing like sand-rubbed copper. They might have been father and son.

Shade reined up, facing them, and saluted with a raised hand. The two men looked at Shade, then at each other, blankly.

"Either of your gents talk American?" Shade asked hopefully.

Maybe they did and maybe they didn't. The blank expressions didn't change. "Well," Shade said determinedly, "I'll just have to do the best I can with what little sign I know." He held out both hands, fingers spread, rotating them three times. Then he made fists of his hands and brought them together. "Friend," he said.

The old man merely stared. The young one grunted and looked bored. Shade optimistically took that to mean that he had been understood. "All right, we'll try somethin' a little harder."

Once more he made the "friend" sign and followed it by drawing his right hand across his forehead, signifying "hat wearer," or "white man." Quickly, he cupped his right hand close to his face and moved it in a circular motion several times, the sign word for "Kiowa."

He was trying to tell them that he had been a friend of Pleasant Potter's, the "white Kiowa." The blank expressions, if anything, grew more blank.

"Pleasant Potter," Shade said, raising his voice, as if hoping to make them understand through sheer volume. "The old man. The Army scout. He married one of your women, if I ain't mistaken. And, if I ain't mistaken again, White Dog's the old man's boy."

None of it was getting through. The two Indians listened

patiently, hunched up on their ponies' withers, but it was clear that they hadn't understood a word. Shade groaned but went on doggedly. "Look, the old man died a little while back and your folks planted him in a cave, up in the Wichitas." He made the "dead" sign, literally "goes under." If it made any impression at all on the Indians, it was only to confuse them.

Then Shade remembered something. "*Ta'pave*," he said, using the only Comanche word he knew.

The two Kiowas sat a little straighter on their blanket pads. Understanding showed in their dark eyes This was the friend of *Ta'pave*. The old one moved his head very slightly. It might have been a nod.

But hold on, Shade warned himself. There's nothin' yet to yell about. "What I want," he said aloud, "is to borrow a horse. Two horses, matter of fact." He held up two fingers and pointed to the restless pony herd. "I'd be glad to pay for them, but I ain't got the money."

That glazed, blank look was coming into their eyes again. "Horses," Shade repeated, almost shouting. "I need the borrow of two of your saddle horses."

The Indians looked at each other and quietly began kneeing their own animals toward the herd. It occured to Shade that they were beginning to understand a little too well. The two men, working quietly but quickly, eased around behind the herd and started it forward. Maybe this "hat wearer" had been a pal of *Ta'pave's*, maybe he hadn't. They didn't aim to lose two good ponies finding out.

Shade could see his transportation slipping away from him. According to Hicks, the place called Hard Fork was at least five miles inside the reservation. A long way to walk, especially with a crippled-up woman to look out for.

"Gents," Shade said regretfully, "I hate to do this, but I'm runnin' short on time. I'll have to insist on the borrow of the ponies." He drew the deputy's rifle from the saddle boot and, with a metallic ring of authority, actuated the lever.

The two Kiowas froze. They gazed with cold eyes at this "friend" of *Ta'pave's*.

Shade rode into the herd and quickly cut out a roan and a mouse dun, the biggest and strongest-looking animals in the bunch. "I got no choice in the matter," he apologized. "I'll send your horses home when I get the chance."

Unarmed, there was nothing the Indians could do. Shade started the two horses toward the creek. Looking back over his shoulder, he saw the two Indians talking heatedly between themselves, and using sign, as Kiowas always did. There wasn't much of it that Shade could make out, but he did see the young one use the sign for "cuts off," slashing his right hand down in front of his lips. It was also the sign for "kill."

II

"You're out of your head!" Horseblanket Mary complained bitterly. "That old sun dancer'll have his whole clan after our scalps before sunup."

"Well," Shade drawled, "I don't aim to stay here and make it easy for them. We'll head out of here soon's it gets dark."

"What difference did it make it they was Kiowa or Comanche?" Hicks wanted to know. "One's mean as the other when you wave a gun in his face."

"No difference at all," Shade admitted, "the way it turned out. But I don't expect they'll come after our scalps. If I don't miss my guess, they'd been out doin' a little borrowin'

164

of their own. From some stockman's corral, or maybe from the *remuda* of some trail herd."

Mary and the deputy dwelled on this for some time. Now that they thought about it, the Kiowas hadn't made much of a fuss over the loss of their two best saddle animals. "Might be somethin' in what you say," the woman admitted. "But that don't mean I'm anxious to head into their reservation right now."

"Suit yourself." Shade grinned thinly. "But sooner or later Allard's hands will flush you out, if you stay here."

Shade staked the livestock in the bottom to graze, then made a closer inspection of the roan and mouse dun. Both animals were iron shod—that in itself ruled them out as Indian ponies. The mouse-colored animal, called *grulla* by South Texans and Mexicans, wore a neat hourglass brand on its right shoulder, the roan a flying A. The brands were unfamiliar to Shade, and he was just as glad that they were.

The deputy walked down from the rock shelf, gazing gloomily at the two horses. Shade pointed to the iron shoes and the brands. "If that ain't enough, look at the hair marks on their bellies where they've been carryin' double-rigged saddles . . . You ever see a saddle-rode Injun horse that didn't have a galled back?" He shook his head, answering his own question. "These animals ain't Injun property."

"We might have a hard time convincin' the Kiowas of that."

"Hell with the Kiowas," Shade snapped. For the first time in almost two years Shade could see a real chance of doing something about Brown. He would allow nothing to interfere with that—not even an Indian uprising.

It was still and hot in the wooded bottom. Shade made his way back to the weed patch to watch for more visitors. The sun, low on the open prairie, was slowly dying, still about an hour high.

What was Allard doing now? he wondered. It was safe to assume that he hadn't stuck long to Bess Durell's false directions. More than likely he had already rounded up some hands to carry out an orderly search of creeks and timber and other possible hiding places.

Shade allowed himself to think about Bess Durell. He found himself looking for reasons not to believe the brutal picture that Mary had drawn of the girl. But he knew that most of it was probably true. Truer, anyhow, than the soft-edged portrait, painted with moonshine and certain gray-haired longings, that Pot Allard carried around in his head.

Shade could almost feel sorry for the rancher . . . if the ghost of old Pleasant Potter hadn't been standing in the way.

When only half the sun showed over the horizon, Shade decided it was time to travel. With Roman Three hands beating the thickets like South Texas brush poppers, their chances would probably be better on the prairie.

Shade fashioned two war bridles from the lead rope—a simple hitch of rope in the mouth and around the lower jaw of each of the new animals. Such a rig could be brutal when used with a heavy hand, but it was the best he could do with what he had to work with. Mary was assigned the deputy's horse, which was too footsore and tired to do any bucking. She also got the saddle. Not, to judge from the almost ceaseless flow of grumbling, that she appreciated the display of chivalry.

They crossed the creek at a well-worn rock bed upstream, maybe one of the old Comanche war trails. From the east bank they gazed uneasily at the rolling prairie. Nothing bigger than a mesquite tree to hide behind, Shade was thinking, if we run into Allard's private posse.

He glanced at Hicks. "You're the one that knows the way. Take the lead."

"I don't like it," Mary complained. "I ought not be ridin', the shape I'm in. Anyhow, it ain't good dark."

"Ride, walk, or stay," Shade said brutally. "I don't care."

III

Joe Hicks, as a lawman, left something to be desired. But he was a better scout than Shade had any right to hope for. He had a farmer's feel for the land, and his intuitions were usually right. At first it seemed that Hicks was rambling aimlessly over the dark prairie, heading in no set direction. But he was only taking advantage of depressions in the reddish earth, the gullies and washes, the shallow valleys that lay between the swells and slopes of the naked rangeland.

If Allard was to find them, he would have to do more than merely watch the ridges. Shade's thin mouth twitched at the corners. Except for the rattling torture of bareback riding, and the never-ending task of keeping the gambling woman from falling out of the saddle, he could have enjoyed these passing moments that brought him closer to Brown's own doorstep.

Once Shade kicked his long-muscled *grulla* and spurted ahead, motioning to the others. In a clump of thorny and perversely graceful mesquite trees, they reined up to let the horses blow.

"I can't ride no more!" Mary gasped. "These busted ribs just about cut the gizzard out of me."

"We ain't far from Hard Fork," Hicks said. "Another ten minutes, maybe." He looked at Shade. "What'd you stop for?"

"To make sure I ain't got a busted tail bone, for one

thing," Shade said grimly. "For another . . ." He nodded at a shaggy knoll at their right. "Ridin' the gullies is fine, but once in a while I like to see somethin'."

Ignoring Hicks' objections and Mary's bitter complaining, Shade slid off the *grulla* and made for the knoll on foot. A moon not much bigger than a ten-cent piece drifted on a dark sky, bathing the prairie with dreamy light. In the distance prairie and sky merged in a grayish haze, and in between were other ghostly knolls.

Far to the north, a minute horseman seemed to rise out of the earth and move with dreamlike slowness along the crest of a rise. Shade watched without blinking for several seconds, and at last man and animal seemed to sink back into the earth.

Far to the east, toward Tribulation, and a little to the south, he glimpsed another figure moving briefly along the crest of a barely noticeable slope. Shade backed down from the knoll.

"They're watchin' the ridges, all right. Looks like Allard might have one bunch of hands sweepin' west from the reservation, and probably another bunch comin' this way from Tribulation. Like circle riders at a roundup."

The deputy swallowed. "They must of passed right over us."

"This time, because we was ridin' the low places. But it shows that Allard means business. If they don't get us this time, he'll just send them back and make them do it over."

Hicks made the sound again, of swallowing. "That Durell girl, maybe she wasn't dealin' off the top to you."

"It's a chance we've got to take." Shade grasped the *grulla's* mane and mounted.

CHAPTER THIRTEEN

I

HARD FORK was a shallow, narrow branch of still another of the many gyp water streams that meandered across the southwest corner of the Territory. The banks, as always, were wooded with cottonwood and salt cedars and willows.

They rode into the speckled play of moonlight and shadow beneath the sparse timber. "This is it," Hicks said. "What do we do?"

Shade eased himself off the *grulla's* back. "The doin's up to Miss Durell."

Mary snorted, climbing down from the deputy's saddle with great effort. "We're aimin' to get our fool selves bushwhacked, if you was to ask me."

Shade and Hicks led the horses upstream and tied them. "I been thinkin' about it," the deputy said worriedly. "Maybe it *is* another bushwhack. Maybe this is the way Allard and the girl schemed it."

"Why did she turn me loose? And why did she send Allard and Tattersall on a snipe hunt when our scalps could have been had for the shootin'?"

An ugly notion crossed Shade's mind. To make sure that none of them escaped, it was possible that Allard had

169

waited to get the three of them together before setting his ambush. Possible, but it lacked the directness of the other murder attempts. Shade was inclined to believe the girl. He kept remembering her indifference to the death of Corry's body. A girl like that wouldn't mind handing her grayhaired sweetheart over to the hangman, especially if it meant getting her hands on that bounty.

"Don't worry about the girl," he said. "If I don't miss my guess, she'll show up just like she said, with Allard on the end of a string, and with all the evidence it takes to hang him."

The deputy clamped his heavy jaws and tramped back to the clearing where they had left the gambling woman.

Mary wasn't there.

A prickling sensation moved up Shade's back. "Mary?" He called quietly but did not move from the dark shadows.

The deputy grabbed Shade's arm. "Where is she?"

Shade gestured for silence. The "clearing," which was mostly a patch of weeds between stands of cottonwood, was no more than twenty feet across. That small area was defined in moonlight—the timber beyond was as dark as a lead bullet. Shade couldn't believe that Mary had deliberately left the clearing to blunder about in the dark timber.

"Mary, where are you!"

The deputy started toward the light, and Shade grabbed him. "Let's find out what happened to the woman before we start invitin' ambush."

Hicks was beginning to sweat. Even in the deep shadow Shade could see his glistening face. "You think it's another ambush?"

"All I know is Mary ain't where we left her, and I ain't anxious to light myself up till I know why."

There was no movement beyond the clearing. Shade tugged his hat off his head and began to scratch. The

170

prickling sensation moved over his scalp. Then—quite sudden-ly—it stopped.

On the far side of the clearing, showing through the grayish, moonlit weeds was what seemed to be a shoe.

With great precision, Shade replaced his hat, took the rifle in both hands and moved slowly back into the brush. The deputy followed, saying nothing, but his breathing was rapid and frightened. Moving quietly, Shade slanted back toward the clearing. Now he could see the object more clearly. It was a shoe, all right. It had a foot in it. Both of them belonged to Horseblanket Mary.

Hicks made a small whistling sound as he exhaled. With a suddenness that startled Shade, the deputy started toward the still figure in the weeds. As he stepped into the moonlit clearing, Shade hissed, "Get back here, you fool!"

It was too late—much too late to help the deputy—and somehow Shade knew it. Instinctively, he twisted back into the brush and threw himself to the ground. The bellow of a big-gauge shotgun shattered the peace of the clearing. Shade, even as he dived to the ground, heard the buck-shot ripping through the brush over his head. He glimpsed the deputy at the instant one of the heavy pellets slammed into his chest. He even heard the small sighing sound that was forced from Hick's throat.

Well, Shade thought grimly, *it looks like Brown means business this time. He's taken that scatter-gun out of hiding.*

He fired once at the point where he had glimpsed the muzzle flash. He rolled quickly to his right, fired two more times, then scrambled back into the brush.

There was no answering blast from across the clearing. Brown was not wasting shells or giving his position away un-til he had a target. Shade concentrated for several long, hard seconds on the fickleness of females. He had no notion why Bess had lined him up for Allard's bullet after first setting him free.

The weeds that grew around the spot where the deputy had fallen were perfectly still. Shade watched them for what seemed a long time. They did not move. Cautiously, he raised himself to his elbows and called, "Allard . . ."

Then he called, "Brown, you're in trouble now." In his mind, the names "Allard" and Brown" were synonymous. "You hear me, Brown. You went and killed yourself a deputy sheriff. No great shakes as a lawman, maybe, but a deputy sheriff all the same. They'll wonder about that, back at the county seat."

The dark timber remained silent.

"Brown, you hear me?"

". . . I hear you, Mr. Shade."

Shade grunted involuntarily. The voice was not Allard's. It was not even a man's voice. It was perversely musical and sounded thoroughly unruffled—it belonged to Bess Durell.

"Are you surprised, Mr. Shade?" She sounded mildly amused.

Shade's face felt strangely stiff. A muscle in his jaw began to jump and he couldn't seem to stop it. Thoughts and impressions clamored for attention—he made himself take them one at a time.

First, that shotgun was at least a ten-gauge. He couldn't see a girl like Bess firing a weapon that size. So Brown was there somewhere. But he wasn't talking. That must mean that he was easing his way around the edge of the clearing, hoping to get a shot at Shade's back.

Bess Durell laughed quietly. "Cat got your tongue, Mr. Shade?"

Dense brush did something to a voice—it was impossible to tell exactly where it came from. He decided to risk a few words while watching the edge of the clearing for Allard.

"Don't you have some questions, Mr. Shade?" She was teasing him now.

"A few," he said flatly. "When a girl, of her own mind, lets go of ten thousand dollars . . . well, it makes a man wonder."

"Does it?" she asked with a kind of remote amusement. "It's simple, Mr. Shade. When we made our deal I didn't know that Mr. Allard aimed on marryin' me." She paused. Shade could almost see her shrug. "Mr. Allard runs fifteen thousand head of beef cattle here on the reservation. Steers, sellin' at twenty dollars or more a head—that don't make your bounty money look like much, does it?"

So she hadn't thought that Allard had meant to marry her. That said a good deal about the opinion Bess Durell had of herself, but it didn't tell Shade what Allard was doing at this particular moment.

"What makes you think Allard will marry you?"

"I asked him," said the voice of wide-eyed innocence, "when he came back from that wild-goose chase I sent him on. I mean, a girl would be a fool not to at least ask, wouldn't she? Mr. Allard bein' so rich and all." There was a smiling pause. "You know what, Shade? He aimed on marryin' me all the time."

Over to Shade's right a clump of weeds moved suspiciously. Or was it just Shade's imagination.

"You can't blame me for turnin' down your bounty money, can you, Shade? You couldn't expect a girl to turn her husband over to the hangman, could you?"

"He ain't your husband yet," Shade reminded her.

But she only laughed. "As good as. Women can most always tell when menfolks are lyin'." She let the statement dangle. "He wasn't lyin', Shade. But I think you was when you promised me all that bounty."

The suspicious bush was perfectly still now. It occurred

to Shade that if he could get Allard to thinking about Bess Durell, he might give his position away.

He said dryly, "I wonder how fast Allard would want you for a wife if he knowed what went on between you and his gunhand?"

Shade watched the brush expectantly, but nothing happened. Nothing moved.

Bess Durell said in a smiling voice, "Not very fast, I guess. But what Mr. Allard don't know won't hurt him."

Shade scowled. Allard was only a few yards away. And he wasn't deaf. What had she meant by ". . . what he don't know won't hurt him"? He *had* to know.

"Tell me somethin' . . ." Shade spoke to Bess, but his eyes probed the dark brush for Allard. "When me and the old scout was first comin' to Tribulation, was it Allard that tried to shoot us out of our saddles?"

"Yes . . . that was Mr. Allard." She sounded almost bored.

"I've been wonderin' about that, after seein' the way he can shoot. He could of killed us both then and there, if he'd been a mind to. Why didn't he?"

"Because," she said, "Mr. Allard's a fool."

Shade blinked. Was this a trick that she and Allard had cooked up to keep him off balance? It didn't seem likely. Neither did it seem likely that Pot Allard would lay out in the dark not turning a hair while the girl he meant to marry called him a fool. "Tell me somethin' else," Shade said. "Was it Allard that killed Pleasant Potter?"

". . . No."

"It was Allard's rifle. I've got the Henry cartridge cases."

Suddenly she laughed. "You're a fool too, Shade. And so was Handsome Corry. Oh, he knowed how to spark a girl, all right, but he was still a fool. He was supposed to kill both of you, and leave some empty Henry shells behind to make it look like Mr. Allard had done it."

174

A coldness settled in Shade's gut. A sense of unreality gripped him.

But something was moving in the brush. The two bodies lying in the dead gray light of the clearing, and the girl opposite him in the timber, and the senseless things she was telling him—all that might have been a bad dream. But the movement in the brush was real.

II

Shade moved very slowly, bringing the dead deputy's rifle to bear on the area of the movement. Now it was still, but somewhere beyond the rim of light a man with a scatter-gun was waiting, watching, listening. Nothing could shock him. Nothing could tempt him to give away his position. Not anger, and not shame.

The temptation was strong to start shooting and hope for the best. But his first shot would expose him—and one answering shot was all a shotgun needed.

A few seconds took a long time passing.

"Shade . . . ?"

From the sound of her voice, Shade could tell that she was frowning. Maybe she was even worried.

That hope made him feel a little better. "I ain't gone anyplace," he said, speaking away from the newly suspected area in order to confuse the source point of his voice. He picked the conversation up where it had trailed off a few seconds before. "You tryin' to tell me that Corry killed the old man on your orders, and tried to make it look like Allard? That don't make much sense, does it."

175

There was another electric silence. Shade sensed that she was getting ready with another shocker.

"Did you hear that, Pa?" she called in an amused tone. "He still thinks you're Mr. Allard. He still thinks Mr. Allard robbed them express folks. How do you reckon a railroad detective could be such a fool?"

If she had wanted to surprise Shade, she had done it. It was hard to believe that a hardscrabble squatter like Whit Durell could be an effective highwayman. It was even harder to believe that his daughter would so coolly give him away. Unless, maybe, she was counting on this piece of news to shock Shade into doing something foolish.

A silence as naked as bones lay briefly on the clearing. Then a black opening appeared in the brush, and the thought flashed through Shade's mind, "Durell or Allard or whoever—he don't figure to draw this game out no longer."

Fire belched from the black wall of timber. The heavy charge seemed to shake the ground that Shade clung to instinctively. No time for thought, no time to act, no time for anything at all except to press as flat as possible and hope. And pray, maybe, in a fit of what trail hands called "bad weather religion."

It seemed to Shade that the muzzle blast went off right in front of his face. With some small, unfrozen part of his mind he was aware of the heavy pellets ripping through the brush, snapping twigs and branches, slamming into tree trunks with the force of hammers.

Shade's moment of panic lasted only a small part of a second. Almost instantly he realized that Pleasant Potter's estimation of Brown had been a true one. Only a greenhorn would fire high, even with a scatter-gun. The professional killer always fired low. If your aim was bad you still had a chance to get your man on a ricochet.

Even before the flash from the muzzled blast had died,

Shade had fired into the red heart of the explosion. A single warning crowded everything else from his mind. Not even a greenhorn was apt to fire high two times running. He fired as fast as he could lever cartridges into the chamber. The ear-punishing bellow of the rifle built up layers of sound that bore down on him like a restraining hand. That's enough, it said. If you haven't hit him by this time, you'll never hit him.

He lay for a moment, breathing as if he had been running. The noise of the shooting moved out of the clearing and into the timber and finally onto the prairie where it died.

Then there was another sound, one the likes of which Shade was in no hurry to hear again. Bess Durell, her voice drawn razor thin by hysteria, was calling to her father.

III

It was a long night—long and hot and soon swarming with mosquitoes from stagnant slews along the creek bottom. Long to the verge of endlessness, and thoroughly miserable.

At first Shade was startled by the Indian quality of Bess Durell's keening. He guessed that one woman was much like another when it came to grieving for father, brother, sweetheart, husband . . . the man she loved more than any other. Several minutes passed before Shade looked at the place where Whit Durell had fallen.

Methodically, Shade studied the still figure of the gambling woman and the deputy. Mary didn't seem to be badly hurt, a small cut and bruise on the left side of her head was all that Shade could find. Not that it mattered now, but Shade figured, from the look of the wound, that Durell hadn't intended to kill her. He had hit her with something, maybe the barrel of his scatter-gun, in order to keep her silent.

Well, Shade thought, she was silent. Maybe her heart had just stopped. Her puffy face, relaxed in death, somehow looked healthier than it had in life. Shade could almost believe that the gambling woman had seen a chance to get a long, uninterrupted rest, and had taken it.

Deputy Joe Hicks' death was absolutely without mystery. A single 0-0 shot had struck his chest and probably lodged in his heart. He never knew what hit him. That would be a great comfort to his wife and kids, Shade thought sourly. At last he brought up the horses and covered the dead faces with his slicker.

A numbing lassitude took hold of him. It seemed that two dead faces were more than enough. He didn't want to look at Whit Durell, but it was something that had to be done, sooner or later. The girl had to be talked to, questioned. Evidence had to be organized, sifted, corroborated wherever possible. It was still hard for Shade to believe that an insignificant squatter could have dealt crippling blows to an outfit like the Grabhorns.

Shade's instinct for survival began to nudge him. Do it now, it said. Before grief becomes hate. Before the girl's hysteria cooled and she regained her usual murderous calm.

Moving across the clearing to the edge of darkness, he searched for the right words. ". . . Miss Durell, I'm sorry."

He had not found the right words. She looked up at him in frozen fury. "You're sorry!" she hissed.

"I never had any choice," he said with dogged reasonableness. "He was trying to blow my head off with that scatter-gun."

She came to her feet, standing rigidly. "What choice do you think my father had? Look at him, Shade! My father. The man you killed. Look at him!" Her voice went shrill.

Involuntarily, Shade glanced at the graceless form. Even in this area of deep shadow he could see the blood glistening darkly. "Look, ma'am . . ."

"A little farmer," she said, as if the words were being forced between her teeth. "That's all he was."

"Not quite," Shade said with coldness of his own. "He was a killer too. And I wish I knew why."

She would have killed him with pleasure if it had been in her power. She stared at him, her eyes dry and hard. After a moment she went on, with words that seemed almost to choke her.

". . . You want to know why! You'll have to go back nearly three years to find the answer to that, railroad detective. Back to that rawhide farm country of lower Kansas —my pa and ma in a wore-out wagon on the mail road north of Caldwell. They was headin' home after sellin' some chickens and early potatoes. The wagon was old, the axle was busted and had been mended with a lick and a promise, the brake shoe was wore through to the wood. The team of mules was spooky and half wild, and my pa had his hands full with the animals when they met the southbound coach . . ."

The edge of hysteria had retreated behind an expressionless mask. She gazed at Shade with an emotion too advanced for hate, and continued in a voice strangely lacking in tone and timber. "They were crossin' a creek on a corduroy bridge. It was May, the month of rain in Kanses, and the water ran almost full bank. My pa saw the coach—he yelled for the driver to wait until he got the team across . . ."

"This was a Grabhorn coach?" Shade asked, when the silence had drawn too thin and taut.

The question penetrated her wall of bitterness. At last she nodded bleakly. "The Grabhorn driver laughed. Said he wasn't holdin' up his run for no dirt farmer. But the jury didn't believe it . . ."

"Jury?" Shade scowled.

"When my pa sued the Grabhorns in court. Nobody wanted to believe him. Or they was afraid to believe him. The driver claimed the stage was on the bridge before Pa's wagon came in sight. The stage, he claimed, had the right of way. He also claimed that my pa couldn't handle his team because he was drunk." She laughed, a glass-hard sound that ended abruptly. "Up till that time Pa had never been drunk in his life."

Shade looked at her in growing discomfort, but she continued with the story before he could speak. "Judge and jury. They were all sorry about the accident, they said. Sorry about my pa losin' his wagon and team. Sorry he'd been banged up some and had been unable to get in his crop that year. Sorry too that my ma had been drowned . . ."

Shade stared.

"Bad luck, they said." Staring back with glittering eyes. "But they couldn't see it was any fault of the Grabhorns. So the judge, he throwed the case out of court, and that was that . . ."

And that was that. Shade sought vainly for something to say. The Grabhorns had won, as they had always won. It had been a minor inconvenience for a while, but now it was over with. So they had thought.

But during those long courtroom arguments Whit Durell had reached a verdict of his own. This time, he decided, the Grabhorns would not get off free. This time they would pay, somehow, for the death of his wife. Money, taken from express cars and coaches, could not bring his wife back—but it might make life a little harder for the Grabhorns. And that was better than nothing.

Shade could understand it now—most of it, anyway. At first it had gone smoothly. Because he hated the touch of

Grabhorn money, he had given it freely to poor farmers like himself, and they in turn had protected him.

But Shade knew that robbers who took from the rich and gave to the poor lived only in stories for children. When Durell accepted Pot Allard's protection and started keeping the money for himself—that was the day he started to die.

Shade heard the sound of horses approaching the fork from the west. But the girl, numb with grief and rage, heard nothing.

"Pa had a right!" she hissed. "Eye for eye, the Good Book says. The Grabhorns killed my ma, didn't they!"

There were no tears in her eyes—they were too filled with hate. She began to shake, as with a chill, and Shade said, "There ain't nothin' to be done right now. I'll build a fire."

The night was hot but the smoke from the fire discouraged the plague of mosquitoes. Shade could not coax the girl into the clearing, but after a while she rose of her own will and huddled in the choking smoke near the fire. Numbness still gripped her. She hadn't thought of a way to vent her hate—and maybe, Shade thought, she never would.

He listened but could no longer hear the horses. Then riders had either veered away from the fork, or were coming in on foot. "I'm a curious cuss," he said. "I can't help wonderin' if Allard knowed about you and your pa. The robberies, I mean."

"I never told him. If that's what you're askin'." She no longer seemed very interested.

But Shade reasoned, Allard must have guessed. He had known, all right, in his own mind. And it hadn't changed a thing. He was still in love with Bess Durell. "Another thing," Shade said, "how did you and your pa aim to tie the express robberies on Pot Allard?"

Her face was twisted, old-looking, almost ugly. "You mentioned it before," he reminded her. "You aimed to make it look like Allard was the robber."

She stared into the fire, and Shade saw that her face glistened wetly. At last there were tears. But could have been caused by the smoke.

"How?" Shade asked quietly.

"I never knowed he aimed to marry me," she said flatly, as if thinking aloud. "There was other men, some rich, and some poor, and some young and full of life . . . like Handsome Corry. All kinds of men, with all kinds of notions about me. But none ever had the notion to marry me before."

"When did you find out?"

She blinked at the fire. "Tonight. A little before dark, when him and Babe Tattersall come back from that crazy chase . . ." She startled Shade by turning suddenly and laughing. It was an ugly sound. "It's funny, ain't it? A rich man like that wantin' to marry Bess Durell. An old man, his hair's all gray. Maybe he would of died pretty soon and all that money would belong to me and Pa . . ."

She dwelled on that thought for a moment, then let it trail off. She was looking again into the fire, speaking her thoughts aloud. "The other men, they'd come out from Tribulation, or maybe from some cattle outfit, but all they had on their minds was a frolic. Sometimes it was different, right at the first, but I never liked menfolks that was down in the mouth and afraid to show a girl a good time. So pretty soon they'd start lookin' at me in a certain way, and the first thing I knowed . . ."

In places like Tribulation, where men were rough and women were scarce, it was easy enough for a girl to get a reputation. But that didn't concern Shade at the moment. "Allard," he reminded her. "How did you and your pa aim to skid him off to the closest hangman and collect that bounty?"

For a long while she did not move or speak. Then, with surprising calm, she turned to Shade. "I guess they would of hung Pa, if they'd of caught him, wouldn't they?"

Shade shrugged. "I guess."

She nodded thoughtfully. "Pa would of hated that, givin' the Grabhorns the last laugh, sort of." Then, without the slightest change of tone, "Pa stuffed some of the express money in the bottom of Mr. Allard's saddle pocket . . ." Something was taking place behind that childlike mask, and Shade was sure that he was not going to like it.

"There's still time," she said. "It's not too late. You can still say Mr. Allard's the one you call Brown. I'll swear it's the truth, and besides there will be the money in his saddle pocket for proof. There's more Grabhorn money back at the soddy. We can divide it up . . ."

But she could see from the set of Shade's jaw that it was no use. "All right." She smiled grimly. "There's another way. We can take that money out of Mr. Allard's saddle pocket with out him knowin' about it. I reckon he'd still want to marry me, if he didn't know about that . . ."

She hesitated, searching Shade's face. There wasn't much hope in those wide eyes now. And not much innocence, either, Shade was thinking. "He's an old man, Shade. A rich old man—he won't last forever. He might not even last the year out."

There it was, finally. A proposal of murder, without a flicker of emotion. She might have been talking about the weather. She waited patiently for Shade's answer, knowing all the time what it would be.

He shook his head slowly from side to side, as if he didn't trust his voice. She sensed that this was her last hand, and she had to play it to the end. "It ain't the money I want, Shade. I want Pa to rest easy now, knowin' that he made the Grabhorns pay for what they did. I could make you a rich man, Shade—when I'm Mr. Allard's widow."

Her eyes promised more than money, but Shade wasn't interested. There was a sickness in his gut. All he wanted now was to have it ended.

He was not surprised when the two men moved out of the brush and stood for a moment at the edge of the clearing. Pot Allard's flat gaze moved over the bodies, touched Shade's face briefly and moved on to Bess. Looking at Bess, he said something to Babe Tattersall, and the foreman turned back to the brush.

"You're a hard man to find," Allard said, speaking to Shade but still looking at the girl. "We was comin' back to make another sweep toward Tribulation when we heard the shootin'."

"I heard your horses a while back," Shade told him. "I guess you heard somethin' besides shootin'."

The rancher nodded. He did look like an old man now— as old as Bess had pictured him. Bess had paled when he and the foreman had first appeared. Once her lips had moved, but she had not spoken.

Tattersall was coming back through the timber. Breaking into the clearing, the foreman shot a mystified look at Bess Durell as he handed something to Allard. It was a drawstring express bag. Even in the moonlight Shade could see the black stenciled word GRABHORN on its side. "Right where she said it was," Tattersall said angrily. "In your saddle pocket."

Allard held the sack but did not bother to open it. He looked tired and gray. At last he looked away from Bess and turned to Shade. "It's over now for you?"

Shade nodded. "Just about."

"I think we better talk before you go."

He turned abruptly and walked across the clearing and

into the timber. Shade hesitated, but curiosity would not let him rest. He followed Allard to the creekbank where dappled light sifted through cottonwood branches, playing on a narrow stream that glistened like polished steel.

IV

Allard said, "I guess you aim to collect that bounty." He stood on the lip of the bank, staring down at the water. "What will you do next? I mean, just how do you go about collectin' blood money, Mr. Shade?"

Shade stiffened but held his temper in check. He wanted to know what was in the rancher's mind. If the game wasn't over, as it appeared to be, he wanted to know about that too. "Well," he said, "in a case like this, the body has to be identified as the body of the express robber. That won't be so hard—there are several express agents that have seen them. Too, there's the Grabhorn money that Miss Durell planted in your saddle pocket, and there's more back at the Durell soddy, she says. There won't be much trouble provin' I've got the right man."

Allard gazed steadily at the bright water. "You're in it just for the money—it don't make any particular difference to you where the money comes from does it?"

Shade scowled. "What do you mean?"

"If I gave you the ten thousand dollars, that would be the same as collectin' the bounty, wouldn't it? You wouldn't have to bother with gatherin' proof and gettin' the body identified."

Shade grunted with surprise. "That girl's played you for a fool. She aimed to frame you and then turn you in for the

185

bounty—you've got the proof in your hand. It never crossed her mind that you aimed to marry her—because she knowed what kind of woman she was, even if you didn't."

"Just the same," Allard said tonelessly, "I'll pay you the full bounty if you leave the body here. Tell your bosses anything that suits you. Tell them the robber lit for Mexico, or he fell in a river and washed into the Gulf."

"It ain't quite that simple," Shade said dryly. "My job goes out the window if I come back without Brown."

Allard turned, peering at him in the faint play of light. When he spoke it was with a tone of finality. "All right. I'll make it twelve thousand. The full bounty price, plus two thousand to hold you over till you catch onto another job."

Shade wagged his head in wonder and disbelief. "After all that girl's done to you . . ."

"That's no worry of yours, Shade!" Then Allard pulled himself up, and set his jaw and spoke quietly. "Twelve thousand, Shade. More money than you've ever seen at one time, most likely."

The silence stretched out as Shade tried to collect his thoughts. "Tell me somethin'. Was it you that first tried to bushwhack me and the old scout the first time?"

Allard grunted. "Yes. But I just wanted to scare you out of these parts."

Shade grinned sourly. "Awhile back Bess called you a fool, and she's right. Folks in Tribulation was your friends, but you hung your spurs in them and rode them into the ground, just because the Durells was afraid they'd start askin' questions. How many friends have you got now? Even your foreman hates your guts—but I guess you know that."

The rancher looked at him but said nothing.

"And I guess you know it was Corry that killed the old scout, but it was Bess that put him up to it. And it was

Bess' notion to scatter empty Henry shells around, makin' it look like you was the bushwhacker."

Allard's face might have been carved from mesquite root. A grinding exhaustion caught up with Shade. He was sick of Allard, sick of the Durells, sick of his job.

Allard said, "The railroad might take you back on when they see that the robberies have stopped . . ."

But Shade knew better. Railroads and express companies didn't take much to excuses. You did the job you were sent to do, or you soon started looking for other work. "Somewheres on this reservation," he said abruptly, "there's a young Injun buck, named of White Dog. Kiowa . . . half Kiowa, anyhow. You know him?"

Allard shook his head, puzzled. "I could locate him, if there was a need."

"And the deputy, Hicks. He's got a family on some hardscrabble squatter outfit up by the count seat. The sheriff could tell you where." A strident voice in Shade's head was harping, *Don't be a fool!* He listened to it, considered it, then slammed the door on it.

Allard was looking at him, wooden-faced, waiting.

Shade took a deep breath and plunged on. "Cut the bounty money up between them. White Dog, and the deputy's woman. The Kiowa will probably take his part in horses —I wouldn't like to hear he'd been cheated."

If Allard was stunned by Shade's requests it didn't show on that wooden mask. "That's all?"

There was Horseblanket Mary, but nothing could be done about her now. "That's all." He watched Allard's frozen expression begin to crack. And Shade sensed that, after all the violence, nothing had really changed for the rancher. He was still in love with Bess Durell. "Lord help you!" Shade told him, then wheeled angrily and tramped back to his horse.

V

It was a long road back from Tribulation. Shade stopped at Fort Sill and telegraphed Division in Baxter Springs. He had the company's outraged reply in his pocket, along with the notice of his discharge.

The numbness was beginning to wear off. Twelve thousand dollars thrown away! Half a lifetime of working for railroads—that thrown away, too. All he had to show for it was a few odd dollars in his pocket, the pack plunder and the two horses. Well, he would have to sell the horses. Then maybe he would catch a stage north. There must be something in Kansas for an ex-railroad detective to do.

His friend the Provost caught him at the trader's corral dickering over the horses. "Story has it you're not with the railroad any more," the Army officer said bluntly.

Shade shrugged. It was a long story and he didn't feel like going into it.

"Another story tells about a shootin' down on the reservation, maybe involving Indians. That would make it Army business."

The two men studied each other. "The old scout's dead," Shade said at last.

The Provost was not surprised. "We heard. He was a great favorite of the Plains tribes—they could cause us more trouble than I'd like to think about, unless . . ." He paused, then went on mysteriously, "Unless somethin' was done about it."

That was putting it rather delicately, Shade thought, remembering how Handsome Corry's promising career as an assassin had been cut off in the bud by White Dog. "I don't expect there'll be any trouble from the Injuns."

188

The Provost considered this and was apparently satisfied. Almost as an afterthought, he said, "We're not as cut off from the world as some folks like to think. Say some young Kiowa buck should suddenly come into a big pony herd— we'd soon hear about it. Or say the widow of some deputy sheriff down in Greer County was to pick up and leave the county with considerable more than she'd entered it with— we'd hear about that, too."

Shade stiffened, but said nothing.

The Provost, in the devious way of a military lawman, abruptly changed directions. "You bought your stage ticket yet?"

Suspiciously, Shade shook his head.

"The Caldwell stage pulls out tomorrow mornin' after reveille. The cowmen up in the Cherokee Strip are organizin' a livestock association. They wanted me to name a man to take charge of the protection end of the outfit. Well, since you wasn't with the railroad any longer . . ." He thrust an official-looking envelope into Shade's hand, turned on one booted heel and strode off across the rock-hard parade.

Shade looked at the letter of recommendation addressed to the Association headquarters in Caldwell. His grin came slowly, but when it came it was untainted by gall. Hates and anger began to leave him, like a fever breaking. Eventually he would be able to think about Pot Allard and feel only a kind of grim pity. He would think occasionally of Bess Durell and hope that Horseblanket Mary had sized her up wrong.

But never again would Shade see one of those wide-eyed squatter girls without wanting to put his back against something solid.

J. R. ROBERTS

THE GUNSMITH

SERIES

An all new series of adult westerns, following the wild and lusty adventures of Clint Adams, the Gunsmith!

☐	30856-2	THE GUNSMITH #1: MACKLIN'S WOMEN	$2.25
☐	30857-0	THE GUNSMITH #2: THE CHINESE GUNMEN	$2.25
☐	30858-9	THE GUNSMITH #3: THE WOMAN HUNT	$2.25
☐	30859-7	THE GUNSMITH #4: THE GUNS OF ABILENE	$2.25
☐	30860-0	THE GUNSMITH #5: THREE GUNS FOR GLORY	$2.25
☐	30861-9	THE GUNSMITH #6: LEADTOWN	$2.25
☐	30862-7	THE GUNSMITH #7: THE LONGHORN WAR	$2.25
☐	30863-5	THE GUNSMITH #8: QUANAH'S REVENGE	$2.25
☐	30864-3	THE GUNSMITH #9: HEAVYWEIGHT GUN	$2.25
☐	30865-1	THE GUNSMITH #10: NEW ORLEANS FIRE	$2.25

Available wherever paperbacks are sold or use this coupon.

◖ ACE CHARTER BOOKS
P.O. Box 400, Kirkwood, N.Y. 13795

Please send me the titles checked above. I enclose $_____.
Include $1.00 per copy for postage and handling. Send check or
money order only. New York State residents please add sales tax.

NAME_____

ADDRESS_____

CITY_____STATE_____ZIP_____

A–1